DEAD MAN'S SWITCH

DEAD MAN'S SWITCH

Sigmund Brouwer

HARVEST HOUSE PUBLISHERS
EUGENE, OREGON

Cover by Left Coast Design, Portland, Oregon

Cover photo © Shutterstock / maigi

DEAD MAN'S SWITCH
Copyright © 2014 by Sigmund Brouwer
Published by Harvest House Publishers
Eugene, Oregon 97402
www.harvesthousepublishers.com

Library of Congress Cataloging-in-Publication Data
　　Brouwer, Sigmund
　　Dead man's switch / Sigmund Brouwer.
　　　　pages cm
　　Summary: On a remote island in Washington's Puget Sound that houses a federal prison where his father works, high school senior King sets out alone to unravel a dark conspiracy after receiving a "fail safe" email from his best friend who drowned in a boating accident two weeks earlier.
　　ISBN 978-0-7369-1747-6 (pbk.)
　　ISBN 978-0-7369-5723-6 (eBook)
　　[1. Mystery and detective stories. 2. Conspiracies—Fiction. 3. Prisons—Fiction. 4. Islands—Fiction. 5. Washington (State)—Fiction.] I. Title.
　　PZ7.B79984Dc 2014
　　[Fic]—dc23
                                                                              2013015454

Printed in the United States of America

　　　　　14 15 16 17 18 19 20 21 22 / BP-CD / 10 9 8 7 6 5 4 3 2 1

Messages can be sent in many ways.

From a method as ancient as a carving on a tree, to lettering in plain view that just needs to be seen in a different light. To binary digits sent through cyberspace. To a video from a friend.

Here's what's different. The messages to King started with emails that his friend sent him two weeks after his friend drowned trying to escape the island.

"Trust no authorities. They will hunt you too."

When King becomes the hunted, he is trapped on the same island, where he can trust no one. Not even his father.

CHAPTER 1

On the morning that King betrayed his father, the white of the clouds was so pure against a blue sky that it almost hurt the eyes, and the crispness of the air and sigh of a breeze among the swaying tops of the spruce gave the illusion of eternal tranquility.

But King felt no tranquility, and he could cling to no illusions. Especially about his father.

In front of King, an arrow-shaped gash on the north side of the spruce tree was the horrible proof. The gash was head high, pointing upward. Exactly as promised in the email that had sent King here. The sap had dried from the gash, trapping a few ants at the edges where gravity had elongated the slowly falling drops.

King had not wanted to find this gash because of what it might mean about the email—and about his father.

Much of the time, especially early in the day, Pacific Coast mist and fog defined the island. It seemed to rise from the waters of Puget Sound yet also descend from the tall spruce on the hills to the rocky shores until, as sentries, the spruce dissolved into a shroud that dampened but didn't completely muffle the low barking of seals gathered at the northern end, where they bobbed and rolled effortlessly in the waves that made the island such a secure prison.

William Lyon Mackenzie King always felt as if the fog were there to taunt him, pressing in as a reminder that the island was a prison that he shared with 103 of the most dangerous criminals in America.

A few hours earlier, King had woken to sunshine slicing through the parted window shades of his bedroom. Much as he hated the fog, his constant enemy, this was a morning when King wished for the fog's presence.

He needed the island mist because if a guard caught him among the trees in the island's forbidden zone, he'd be unable to spin or charm or bluff his way out of the situation with the creative dialogue that usually left adults—except his father—shaking their heads at him with cheerful resignation.

But it was more than that.

A son should not betray his father.

King had been able to sneak to this location because of a hack into the prison's infrared scanning system that prevented it from detecting his body heat. It hurt King inside to think that by sneaking to this location on the island, he was trusting a hacker rather than believing his father was innocent.

So as much as he hated the fog, King wanted it to surround and hide him because he was about to commit an act of shame. A son should not betray his father.

*

It wasn't too late. If he walked away now, there would be no betrayal, no disloyalty. He felt as if he were swaying at the edge of a rooftop on a high building, knowing the consequences of the next and final step.

If a son truly had faith in his father, he wouldn't need to prove that his father was innocent of a crime the world did not yet know existed. A son with faith in his father would turn around and leave the forbidden zone.

But if his father was innocent, why hadn't King been surrounded by armed guards by now?

King didn't like the answer. It could only mean the email had been accurate when it promised that the prison's computer system would shut down the infrared scanners for two hours.

Which meant something frightening about the remainder of that email message. It meant his father had already betrayed him.

CHAPTER 2

King stood on one of the slopes overlooking the cleared flatland where the worst offenders in the US prison system were locked in buildings surrounded by an electric fence. The barbed wire bounced silver sunshine at him in the middle of the first sunny morning of the week.

Tilting his view away from the shiny silver strands of lethal wire, he looked beyond at the snow-covered peaks of the Olympic Mountains, so often hidden in the island fogs. On too-rare days of sunshine like this, the peaks reminded King that only a few miles of frigid and deep channel waters separated McNeil Island from Tacoma. Men had been imprisoned on this island for more than a century, and it was the cold water that kept them prisoners. The unpredictable tidal currents of the sound were dangerous enough, but an escapee's body could not withstand the hypothermia that would set in long before he swam halfway to the mainland.

This century's inmates were too dangerous to be allowed to roam the island. They never saw the Olympic Mountains. Instead, they saw concrete blocks painted smooth, inch-thick bullet-proof glass, and massive doors that slid sideways only if the correct password was punched into an electric lock from the main control room by guards who surveyed every movement by surveillance cameras. The password was changed each day, and when a door slid open, it revealed another door because every cell and every hallway had two doors with a five-foot gap between, and only one door could be opened at a time.

As King placed his hands on the thick branch near his head, he saw the occasional flit of black and gray as chickadees fluttered from branch to branch above him. He was nearly at maximum elevation on the island—315 feet. He heard the chickadees, the whistling of wind in the branches, and the occasional throbbing diesel engine of a fishing trawler out of sight somewhere in the channel. The inmates only heard the hush of air moving from the narrow vents in the ceiling because they were each completely isolated. If they did hear human screams, the sound came from themselves. Not screams of fear, but rage.

Except for the prison and the homes for the 40 federal prison employees and their families, McNeil Island was essentially pristine, pure, and uncontaminated. No regularly scheduled ferry service. All transportation to and from the island was strictly controlled by the prison authorities. No stores. No services. No school. Three-quarters of the island was a wildlife refuge—untamed, unbroken.

Because of this isolation, McNeil Island, with its hills and coastline and freshwater reservoirs and patches of pasture and farmhouses built with neat fussiness, was just as much a prison for King as for the 103 convicts.

Yet it was less than a ten-minute helicopter ride away from where King yearned to be. In a hospital at the side of his mother, Ella, who was in a coma. Alone. Among the millions of people of Tacoma and Seattle who worried about traffic jams and getting their Starbucks order placed correctly, mostly unaware of how close they were to these violent convicts, unaware of the infrared scanners and other security systems that guarded the forbidden zone.

King wasn't allowed to know why any of the men had been placed inside the prison. Too violent, too scary, he'd been told, and absolutely none of his business as a family member of a prison employee.

And he most certainly was not allowed to be in the forbidden zone above the complex of prison buildings.

* * *

If the instructions in the email were correct, King had only 20 more minutes of protection from the infrared scanning alarms. He glanced at his iPhone GPS for one final confirmation of his location.

The coordinates showed him at a longitude of 47° 12' 40" N and a latitude of 122° 41' 20" W. He'd been sent to this location by someone who had reached out to him from beyond the grave. With a message to find a package hidden in a tree. A tree in the island's forbidden zone.

King peered upward. If something was waiting there for him, he didn't want to find it. Because that would mean yet another part of the email was accurate. The part about his father. The same father who would not let King go to the hospital on the other side of the water to be with Ella and hold her hand and tell her stories in case she could hear something behind the eyelids that wouldn't even flutter with any signs of real life.

If something was waiting there for him, he didn't want to find it. But he had no choice. King began to climb.

CHAPTER 3

The metal and glass of the black iPhone, slim and sleek even in comparison to the generations of iPhones that followed, weighed only 3.95 ounces—112 grams. But as King stepped into the schoolroom that afternoon, the phone felt like a bulky hand grenade in his right front pocket, heavy as lead.

A quick glance showed him that everyone else in the homeschool co-op was already there. Ten kids, ranging from first grade all the way up to where King had been placed, a senior in high school. His placement wasn't because of his age, but because he'd ripped through the curriculum over the past years. King wanted out of school. Until two weeks earlier, all he'd really wanted was freedom. Now what he really wanted was for his mom to wake up and smile and come back to their home.

King never showed fear or pain. That was one of his codes. Because of the iPhone in his pocket, he was almost overwhelmed by both of those emotions, but he hid them well.

He smiled and waved all around as kids looked up and greeted him. The windows showed that fog had returned. Normally, there would be a view of the other buildings in this corner of the island. Half were empty farmhouses now. The largest prison area had been shut down, leaving only high-security buildings, so only a third of the families were left on the island.

King walked through the room. He was glad the instructor brought in from Tacoma was late for the weekly writing class. With only unscheduled ferry service to the island, class didn't always start on time. King needed this time to talk to Mike Johnson.

King moved to his usual place beside Johnson, who was sketching out a dragon in a notepad at his own desk. Mike was tall, gangly, and working hard on a mustache. Even though Mike's hair was dark, the mustache took some imagination to visualize. The week before, Samantha, one of the seven-year-old girls in the co-op, had innocently offered Mike a damp cloth to wipe the dirt off his lip.

"Kinger," Johnson said in the groovy, cool way he liked to use as he talked. Johnson was the only one who thought it was groovy or cool. Some days—and King felt bad for it—he wondered if he and Johnson would be friends if they were not forced to be together on the island. As the only two guys their age among the prison-employee families on the island—now that Blake Watt was dead—King didn't have many choices for friends.

"MJ," King responded.

"Hey," Johnson said. "Any word on your mom?"

King could see the concern in Johnson's eyes, and he knew Johnson wasn't asking just to be polite. It made King instantly regret his semi-traitorous thought about whether he and Johnson would be friends off the island.

"Still the same," King said. "It's good news and bad news, right?"

King's mind flashed to the memory of seeing Ella in a hospital in Seattle. In an extended-care wing of a hospital. Being fed with intravenous tubes because of the unexpected stroke that put her in a coma. And with that flash of memory came the usual anger that she was alone. ALONE.

"Dude," Johnson said. "Anything I can do to help, I will. Okay?"

"Help with this." King pulled the iPhone from his pocket and sat. He slid the iPhone to Johnson. "Seen it before?"

King reached over and hit the home button so the lock screen photo showed.

Johnson's eyes widened, just as King had expected. In clear techno color, the screen showed a jack of spades.

"This was Blake's," Johnson said. "Unless somebody copied his wallpaper."

"Check out the back."

Johnson flipped it over and ran his finger across the top edge, as King had also expected. When King and Johnson had delivered the phone to Blake, Blake had freaked out at a nick in the bevel. Blake had refused to calm down when they pointed out that you couldn't expect perfection from an eBay purchase, but it hadn't mattered. They hadn't known Blake long, but by then, they did know he was a freak about details.

"Yep, Blake's," Johnson said.

Which meant it was the iPhone that King and Johnson had smuggled onto the island for Blake. The one they had lied about to the prison warden after Blake had drowned. Lied repeatedly.

Johnson also whispered the question King expected. "Where did you find it?"

In a tree, King thought but did not say. In a tree, following instructions from an email that Blake sent yesterday. Which was impossible because Blake had drowned in Puget Sound, and they'd already had his funeral. Blake had drowned trying to do what King wanted to do—escape the island. But King didn't want to die in the process.

King didn't answer Johnson's question about where he'd found the iPhone. Too complicated right now. He didn't want Johnson freaking out just before class started.

"Check this out," King said.

He reached over again and moved the slider to take the device from lock screen to home screen.

Four blank squares appeared across the center. Below was a touchscreen keypad. Above was the phrase "Enter password."

King remembered the email instructions that had been sent the day before from a friend who had drowned two weeks earlier: "MJ knows the password. Four wrong tries and all the data is gone."

"I don't want anything to do with this," Johnson said. He looked around, as if expecting the warden to step into the room and confront them. "Throw it away."

It's what King wanted to do. And he would have done, but the email had told King that if he didn't follow instructions, the world would find out about a crime that King's father had committed.

Johnson slid the phone back to King. "We can't get caught with this. You know all those rumors about Blake being a hacker. You know what will happen to us if anyone finds out we got this for Blake."

CHAPTER 4

King held the iPhone in place, keeping the screen activated so Johnson had to look at it. Johnson couldn't take his eyes off the blank squares, as if the device were a deadly cobra, hypnotizing him.

"What's the password?" he asked Johnson, pointing at the empty squares. "According to Blake, you're supposed to know it."

"What, Blake has been talking to you like a ghost?"

"That's not the point. What's the password?"

"No," Johnson said. "I don't know it. And even if I did, I'm not getting involved. You heard what they told us last week. If they—"

Johnson put a fake smile on his face as he looked past King. "Sammer," Johnson said in his cool and groovy voice.

A small hand touched King's shoulder. He knew it was Samantha. Seven years old. Blonde. Very shy. Missing her front teeth.

King turned to her and saw tears. "Can you help me with my math tables?" she asked. The "s" at the end of "tables" whistled a bit because of her missing teeth.

King smiled. He was nearly overcome by the fear of being caught with Blake's phone, the pain of learning this horrible thing about his father, and the ache of being separated from his mother, but here was a problem he could handle.

"Let's start with the nine times," King said. "Hold up your hands with your fingers open."

She did.

"One times nine," King said. He reached out and folded down her pinky. "How many fingers now?"

Samantha counted. "Nine. One times nine equals nine."

"Yep," he said. "Fingers up again."

She did.

"Two times nine. Fold down this finger. The second one."

He touched the finger beside her pinkie. She bent the finger.

"Excellent," King said. "How many fingers on this side?" He pointed at the pinkie.

"One," she said.

"And on the other side of your folded finger?"

She frowned in concentration. "Eight."

"One. Eight. That's eighteen. Two times nine is eighteen."

"I get it," Johnson said. He held out his own hands. "Three times nine." He folded down his third finger. "Two fingers on one side, and seven on the other. Twenty-seven. Cool."

It didn't take much to amuse Johnson, King thought. It was one of the things he liked about Johnson.

"Try this," King said to Samantha, touching the thumb on her other hand. "Jump to six times nine."

Samantha counted to six and folded down the thumb on her second hand. "Five on one side, and four on the other."

"Fifty-four!" Johnson's voice rose in triumph. "Ha!"

"I'm the one who's supposed to be learning this," Samantha said in a grave voice. At least she wasn't crying anymore, King thought, even though her nose was still runny.

"It works for all the nine times tables," King said. "I don't have any tricks for the others, but once you learn this, you'll know you can learn more. Okay?"

Before Samantha could answer, the door to the room slammed shut. "I expect everyone to be in their desks when I arrive," said the instructor. "Especially when the ferry has delayed me and given you plenty time to be ready."

David Raimer. Never "David" and never "Raimer," as he had warned them on his first day. Always "Mr. Raimer."

Raimer continued in the same irritated voice. "I've made that very clear."

He was a large man who shaved his head. He wore rimless glasses, which King suspected he did not need, and a black sport coat above his blue jeans. He worked hard at looking like an author and talked end-lessly about the one book he published. This one book had ensured he could get paid the big bucks to travel once a week from Tacoma to the island to teach the homeschool kids.

Kids scurried into place as Raimer smiled at their obvious fear.

He looked at his desk at the front of the room. "I want the adverb worksheets I asked you to complete."

He looked around, waiting for a response. No one moved.

"Well?" he said. "What's taking you?"

"Difficult to hand them in when we're supposed to stay in our desks," King said.

No one laughed. During the previous weekly classes, Raimer had managed to install drill-sergeant discipline. And seemed proud of it. "Don't give me any back talk," he said.

King got up. Without his worksheet.

"Sit," Raimer said. "Until I'm ready to ask for the worksheets."

King was tired of Raimer and the drill-sergeant routine. King didn't sit. Maybe if he hadn't been in a bad mood because of the iPhone that belonged to a friend who had drowned, it would have been different. King defied Raimer and moved to a counter at the side of the room.

"I said, *sit!*" Raimer was easily six inches taller than King, and King was tall for his age.

King ignored Raimer and took a tissue box off the counter. He moved back toward his own desk but stopped by Samantha, pulled out a tissue, and smiled.

"If you kiss your honey when your nose is runny," King told her, "you may think it's funny, but it *snot*."

He wiped her nose.

Only then did he sit. If Raimer was proud of the instant silence he could generate, King was proud that a few kids had broken the silence to giggle at the joke.

"No more warnings," Raimer told King. "Anything else and you're gone."

King realized at that moment just how tired he was of this guy pushing everyone around. He was in a really bad mood because of the iPhone and the reason he had it. Lately, he'd woken in a bad mood every day because Ella was on the mainland. And his dad, Mack, didn't seem to care that she was ALONE.

King stood.

"Sit," Raimer barked.

King remained standing. He lifted a piece of paper from his desk.

"Here's my adverb worksheet," King said. "I can tell you, sir, that I believe it was not only a waste of time, but a bad thing to teach us."

King ripped the sheet into strips.

The silence felt like a showdown at noon in a Western movie. King folded the strips neatly and tucked them into his pocket. Alongside the iPhone that a dead friend had asked him to retrieve from a tree in the forbidden zone.

"You're gone," Raimer said. "I'll be reporting this to the warden."

Yep, King realized, he was tired of Raimer. And in a bad mood that was only going to make this situation worse. But he wanted a fight. Any kind of fight would feel better than what he was feeling.

"Sure," King answered. "Is that because you're afraid I'm right and you're wrong? Or is it because you need to hide behind the warden like a little boy hiding behind his mom's skirt?"

CHAPTER 5

"I've changed my mind," Raimer said. "You can stay long enough to apologize. After that, you can leave."

"Here's the pitch," King said. He pretended he was holding a microphone to his mouth. "And the crack of the bat…folks, he just hit that ball hard. Wow, it's moving quickly through the air."

"Have you lost your mind?" Raimer asked.

"Sports commentators get paid because they are great with words," King answered. He'd already drawn Raimer into an argument, and Raimer didn't seem to realize it. "You never hear them talk like that. Hit the ball *hard*? Moving *quickly*? 'Hard' and 'quickly' are adverbs, and commentators stay away from adverbs. I started to think about this as I worked through all the lame adverbs on the worksheet."

King put the imaginary microphone back to his mouth. "Here's the pitch…and the crack of the bat…folks, he *pounded* that one into left field!"

King paused. "Folks, he *sniped* it between the shortstop's legs. He *lasered* it over first base. He *crushed* it over the fence. Better yet, folks, he *mashed* it over the fence. 'Sniped,' 'lasered,' 'crushed,' 'mashed.' Those are great verbs. And when you have a great verb, you don't need help from an adverb. So why teach us to use adverbs if that's teaching us to use weak verbs?"

Raimer open his mouth to say something. Then shut it. Then opened it. Then shut it. Then opened it. "I'm not teaching you this—the curriculum is."

"So you are a teacher of curriculum, not a teacher of kids?"

As if he'd found his safe spot, Raimer glared and raised his voice. "I'm paid to follow the curriculum that the homeschool course puts in front of me."

"Not to teach us to be good writers?"

"You've had a bad attitude since I arrived," Raimer said. "I think you have some serious personal problems, and you need to learn to deal with them."

Johnson stood. "Pulverized."

Raimer gaped. Johnson had always seemed to be afraid of Raimer.

"Kinger," Johnson whispered. "I've got your back."

King felt a sudden warmth for his friend and knew in that moment that they really were friends and that he'd miss Johnson if they weren't on the island together. Johnson spoke out to Raimer again. "'Pulverized.' That's a great verb too. Here's the pitch…the crack of the bat… he *pulverized* the ball! That's better than him saying he hit the ball really hard or it moved quickly."

"So that's two of you I can suspend?"

King was amazed that Johnson had dared to defy Raimer, and he was touched that Johnson was so loyal, but he didn't want Johnson in trouble.

"Sir," King said, drawing the heat back to himself, "If one thing is wrong about the curriculum, then what else is wrong about it? If you can't trust authorities in one thing, why should you trust them in anything?"

Saying it, King couldn't help think about the email that sent him to a spruce tree with a gash on the north side. About how he could no longer trust his own father.

"This insolence staggers me," Raimer snarled.

"See," King said. He knew he was in so much trouble that it didn't matter how much further he went. "'Staggers.' That's a great verb. Didn't need an adverb."

"Obliterated," said Evelyn, an eleven-year-old girl, as she stood. "Here's the pitch…the crack of the bat…he *obliterated* the ball!"

King hid his smile. The revolt had just gained momentum.

From her desk, Samantha asked, "What does 'ovliterate' mean?"

"Hit so hard that you destroy it," Evelyn said. "I think King is right. Adverbs are weak. Strong verbs are way more fun."

Raimer blinked in disbelief at the growing rebellion.

"'Ovliterate' is a great one!" Samantha said, struggling to say "obliterate" through the gap in her teeth. "Like on the mainland when we are driving on the highway and a bug hits our windshield. It gets ovliterated. The guts are splattered. Yellow and green everywhere. And when my dad uses the windshield wiper, he smears the guts and then says bad words."

Samantha giggled. "'Splattered' is a great verb too, right?"

King gave her the thumbs up, and all the other students applauded.

"Enough!" Raimer shouted. He pointed at King. "I want you out of this class right now."

"What a coincidence," King said. "That's exactly what I wanted."

CHAPTER 6

"Think your dad is going to go crazy because you got kicked out of class?" Johnson asked King.

A couple of hours had passed since King had walked out of class. They stood in a shadow on the eastern shoreline, just the two of them. The trees behind them had begun to hide the afternoon sun. The vague mildewy salt smell of low tide was a tang in every breath King took. Green crusted rocks were exposed that at high tide would be ten feet underwater. Small creatures in the shallow tidal pools darted from one hiding spot to another, sending ripples that betrayed their fear. King could sympathize. If he thought that scurrying from one hiding spot to another would solve his problem, he'd be fine risking some ripples.

"If you had to swim it, what do you think?" King asked Johnson. He had no intention of talking about his dad. First, because of the iPhone and what it might mean. Second, because he and his dad barely talked anymore, ever since The Coma and the fact that Ella was ALONE. That's how it always appeared in King's mind—The Coma. There hadn't been much else to think about since The Coma. Nothing much else in the household had seemed to matter with just King and his dad in the empty house. Now, however, King had a new worry. Blake Watt's iPhone.

Johnson followed King's gaze. A few miles across Puget Sound was the western edge of Tacoma.

"It would be great to get rid of Raimer, wouldn't it?" Johnson said.

"Think you could swim it?"

"Oh, I get it," Johnson said. "You don't want to talk about Raimer."

"So little gets past you," King said. He paused. "If someone was hunting you on the island, could you make it across?"

"Ask the last prisoner who tried," Johnson said. "Oh wait, he drowned. Or ask Blake. Oh wait, we just had his funeral because he flipped his boat."

"No life jacket. And he couldn't swim. How about you?"

"I like standing. I can't do that on water."

"Could you make it across if you had to?"

"You know how dangerous the currents are," Johnson said. "And the cold water will get you if the currents don't. There's a reason the prison was put on this island. What has gotten into your brain?"

"An email," King said. He pulled Blake Watt's iPhone out of his pocket. "The one that sent me to this."

"Throw it in the water!" Johnson said. Not joking.

King knew why, of course. This was the device they had already lied about repeatedly to the warden, to their parents, to Blake's parents. It was one of those small white lies that had grown and grown. After the first denial, telling the truth became increasingly difficult.

"I might," King said. "But let me tell you about the email."

"No," Johnson said. "This is how you drag me into things. You make it sound little at first, and then before I know it, we're in the middle of something that you knew all along was going to be big."

"There's a reason I do that," King said. "If I told you what I had in mind, you'd never take that first step. There's a bird they named after you. It rhymes with micken, and it sounds like this. *Bawk, bawk*."

King flapped his arms as if they were wings and expected Johnson to smile. It didn't work.

"I'm out of here," Johnson said. He turned to go up the path.

"Give me the password first," King said. "That's all I need."

"One two five eight."

"How difficult was that?" King said. "Thanks. See ya."

Johnson disappeared into the narrow path that led through the trees, away from the shoreline.

King hit the home button and the four square boxes came up. He touched the number pad to input the digits. One. Two. Five. Eight.

The screen flashed a red banner across the top with the words, "Wrong password." The squares remained empty blanks.

"Hey!" King shouted. He spun and ran up the path after Johnson. "Hey!"

He caught up to Johnson at the gravel road that ran parallel to the shoreline a hundred yards inland.

"That's not the password," King said. Mad.

"Oh, so sorry," Johnson said. "I made a mistake. It's five nine two three."

King tried it. The phone screen flashed again.

That was two tries. Only two left. Blake's email said he had tweaked some software on the phone. Apple gave you six attempts and then made you wait a minute to try again. Blake had apparently tinkered with that to make it more secure.

"Or maybe nine three three three. So many choices. Or eight eight two three."

"So you're just giving me random numbers."

Johnson shrugged. "Normally you figure things out faster than that. After all, you are the Lyon King."

It was obvious that Johnson was as mad at King as King was at Johnson. King rarely lost his temper, but right now he was tempted to see if he could fit the iPhone down Johnson's throat. Sideways.

"This is serious," King said. "The email said—"

"I don't care what the email said," Johnson told him. "We made a big mistake getting Watt the iPhone. We lied just to buy it and deliver it. And we knew it was wrong when we did it. I told you then and I'll tell you now. When someone pays you two thousand dollars for something that's barely four hundred, there has to be a catch. Especially when the kid is only fourteen and shouldn't have that kind of money. Oh, and let me think…especially when his parents started asking about it after he was gone."

"We didn't know about the hacker rumors until after," King said. It was a weak argument, but it was the best he had.

"Well, we know now. We were idiots to get it for him. Why wasn't Blake supposed to have computer access? And that, Kinger, was a rhetorical question. I don't want to know what Blake was doing with the phone, but it can't be good. Go back down to the rocks and throw it in the water."

"Okay," King said.

"Okay?" Johnson was instantly suspicious.

"If you let me tell you about the email. Then I'll let you decide."

Johnson groaned. "Why do I know I'm going to regret this?"

"The email said, 'Trust no authorities. They will hunt you too.' That's why I was wondering about the chances of swimming to the other side."

"That's the perfect way to get your attention," Johnson said. "You love not trusting authority."

King took a deep breath to do his best to remain patient. "Mike," he said, "the email came from Blake. You know, Blake Watt. It was sent to me yesterday morning. But we both know he drowned. We were at his funeral. His parents have already moved off the island."

"Someone pretended to be him. Playing a joke on you."

"And shutting down the infrared scanners so I could go into the forbidden zone and find the iPhone? Those rumors about Blake being a hacker...maybe they were true. Remember that it was such a big deal that he wasn't allowed on computers?"

"Forbidden zone?" Johnson's eyes widened. Any kid on the island understood how significant that was. Thermal sensors were set everywhere. If a prisoner actually managed to escape the prison building, cross the electric fence, and scamper into the rugged nature preserve that made up three-quarters of the island, his body heat would give away his location, and the sensors would track his every movement.

King told Johnson about the GPS coordinates and finding the iPhone duct taped to the trunk of a tree, about 20 feet up.

"So someone is messing with you big time. Dead people don't send emails," Johnson said.

"Did you send it?" King asked Johnson.

"Right. And I hacked into the prison computer system to shut down the scanners."

"Then it was Blake. The email outlined in detail how we had

purchased the iPhone and smuggled it onto the island. It mentioned the nick in the bevel. Only three people knew. You. Me. And Blake."

"And the email was dated yesterday? Not before he drowned? Maybe you missed seeing it before."

"Yesterday. Think I didn't look at the date and time on it 15 times to make sure?"

"Dead people don't send emails," Johnson said.

"Yes they do," King said. "It's called a dead man's switch."

CHAPTER 7

Before continuing with his explanation, King glanced at his watch. In 20 minutes, they needed to be back at their own houses for the six p.m. head count. It wasn't exactly a curfew, but close enough. Since Blake had drowned, all family members of prison employees needed to be accounted for three times a day.

"Dead man's switch," King repeated. "It's a fail-safe thing. Like with a forklift. If the driver goes unconscious for any reason and his foot leaves the gas or the brake, it automatically shuts off."

"Blake spent a lot of time on forklifts."

"Shut up," King said. He never spoke like that. It got Johnson's attention, and the smirk on Johnson's face died. "The switch is usually wired to break a circuit. It protects locomotives, tractors, chainsaws, a bunch of things like that."

Johnson nodded, but King could tell he had hurt Johnson's feelings. He would get around to fixing that later. This was too important.

"Sometimes," King said, "the dead man's switch is not meant to protect, but to threaten. Like for hand grenades. Once the pin is pulled, when someone lets go of the handle to throw it, the switch activates a circuit and the countdown begins to the explosion. A bank robber goes into a bank holding a live grenade, and if somebody takes him down, the grenade goes off. But as long as he's holding the handle against the side of the grenade, nothing goes wrong."

"If I say anything or ask anything, are you going to yell at me again?"

King shook his head. "You just need to take me seriously. I'm scared."

"Scared? I've never seen you scared." Now Johnson looked worried.

"No, you've seen me scared plenty. I just hate showing it. So look at me. I'm scared."

"Still look the same," Johnson said, trying a grin. "And I don't want you scared. Because then I'll get scared."

"You'll get over it. You're scared all the time."

"I know. Now tell me the rest. This isn't about locomotives or chainsaws or hand grenades."

"You get the concept, right? The switch is in place to set something off if the person in control of the switch loses control."

"Loses control. As in—"

King didn't let Johnson finish. He didn't like the word "dead." He didn't even like saying it to explain a dead man's switch. His mother suddenly was in a coma and might die at any time. Nothing had changed King or his father more than that. Kids around him didn't really understand. To them, dead was what happened to SpongeBob SquarePants or to Wile E. Coyote when he chased the roadrunner in Bugs Bunny cartoons. Horrible, violent things happened to Sponge-Bob or to the coyote, but a second later, they were put back together and doing cartoon things again.

To King, dead was imagining what it might be like to touch his mother's face in a casket, expecting her skin to be soft and warm and waiting for her to open her eyes and smile. To King, dead was watching his father stand in the open front door of their house every night, looking out into the darkness in utter silence as if King didn't exist in the kitchen behind him, just as lonely.

"There are websites," King said. "One of them is even named Dead Man's Switch. What happens is you put stuff into an email or a bunch of emails. And if you don't go to the website once a day—or whatever frequency you set up—and put in a password, the emails start going out automatically."

"Obviously then, Blake set this up before…" Johnson didn't finish the sentence. He was beginning to believe in the reality of this situation. Slowly. The same way King had. "How do you know about all this?"

"Didn't take much," King answered. "Just a few Google searches.

I checked it out after the first email from Blake. Wiki told me about switches in general, and then I googled for more specifics. That's when I took the instructions in the email seriously."

Johnson let out a big sigh. "There. You've done it. Given me just enough to drag me into whatever you're doing. Now I have no choice but to ask."

King waited.

"What did the email say?" Johnson asked.

King reached into his pocket. He had been waiting for this moment. To not be alone. He took out a piece of paper and unfolded it.

"I'll read it to you as we're walking," King said. "Otherwise we miss head count."

"Yeah," Johnson said. "Like we need that reminder about Blake at this point."

King held the paper and read aloud.

> King, if you get this, it means I'm probably dead. SOMETHING CRAZY AND INSANE BAD IS HAPPENING AT NIGHT. TRUST NO AUTHORITIES. THEY WILL HUNT YOU TOO. Print this out and then immediately trash this email and empty the trash on your computer. It might not make a difference because if they find out about this, they can get on the servers and find a copy. So this will be the last email you get from me this way. Everything else will be untraceable. To get the next messages, you're going to need the iPhone. The coordinates are 47° 12' 4" N, 122° 41' 20" W. The tree will have a long wide gash on the north side, about head high. The tree is in the forbidden zone. Once you click on the link in this email, there will be three short windows of time when the infrared scanners will be blocked by a program that I slipped into the prison mainframe: 9 to 11 the morning after you click the link and 9 to 11 each of the two mornings after that. After you get the iPhone, go to Johnson. MJ

knows the password. Just ask him about The Room.
I've rigged the phone. Four wrong tries and all data is
gone. You will get further instructions from the iPhone
after you unlock it.

As King folded it, he was too aware that the bottom of the page was torn. He'd done it, not daring to leave the remainder of the email anywhere in existence.

A more cautious person would have burned the paper after finding the iPhone in the tree. But King wanted to be able to show it to his dad if he was caught in the forbidden zone. He didn't care about anyone else on the island being mad at him. Just his dad.

But King couldn't leave the remainder of the email on the piece of paper for his dad to read. The next part detailed how King and Johnson had smuggled an iPhone to Blake for $2000. That part of the email would have disappointed his dad, and King hated disappointing his dad.

And King didn't want his dad to see the part that really scared him, now that everything else in the email had been correct. It was the part that said if King didn't retrieve the iPhone from the tree and unlock it within 72 hours, another set of emails would begin reaching the websites of every local radio and television station and newspaper with information about a serious crime that involved King's father—the crazy and insane bad thing happening at night on the island.

Johnson asked King to read the email aloud twice more. They were now less than five minutes from the cluster of picture-perfect farmhouses on the picture-perfect island. The last of the sunlight was glowing warm, and fingers of shadows seemed to caress them as they walked down the road.

"What I don't get," Johnson said, "is why you'd take the chance that the email was right about the infrared scanners being blocked? Yeah, you can believe it came from Blake after you learned about a dead man's switch. But why believe the rest of it? Like that the infrared scanners had been blocked? I mean, really, you think Blake could have arranged something like that?"

"I had my reasons." Like, King thought, the threat to expose whatever crime his father had committed.

Johnson stopped and put a hand on King's shoulder. "Sorry, Kinger. I'm not going any further on this. You asked me to listen to what the email said, and if I did, you said you'd get rid of the phone. I listened. Get rid of it."

"I didn't tell you everything about the email," King said. "There's a part I tore off the page. And it's the reason I went into the forbidden zone. It said if we didn't continue, the media would find out that my dad was part of the crazy and insane bad thing happening at night on the island."

"It's a bluff," Johnson said. "Your dad? Ha. Everyone knows he's rock-solid honest."

King wasn't prepared to test their friendship. He wasn't prepared to ask Johnson to help him prove whether it was a bluff. He didn't want to know if their friendship was strong enough for Johnson to risk all the danger that might be ahead of them just for King and his father. So King prepared himself to look squarely into Johnson's face and lie. He would tell Johnson the truth after they figured out the password.

"Mike," King said, knowing that he was about to betray his friend by lying, just as he had betrayed his father by believing the email and looking for the iPhone in the tree. "The email also said your father was part of the stuff happening on the island. If we don't get to the next set of instructions before the deadline, the world would learn about his involvement too."

CHAPTER 8

King's dad was Mackenzie William King—Mack to everybody, including King, who'd been calling his dad Mack ever since King could swing a small baseball bat at the lobs that Mack had loved tossing in the backyard of their small home.

Some 20 years earlier, at a friend's wedding, Mack had met a Canadian girl named Ella Hutchison, a cross-border cousin of the bride. Mack had a reputation then for fighting hard and driving hard, and most people thought it was only a matter of time until his way of living took him into prison. The chance meeting at the wedding had changed things. The instant, utter, crazy, hopeless love at first sight had become family legend. Mack told that to everyone. And after a pause, he added, "She chased me and chased me until I also fell in love with her."

Everyone laughed at that. Ella, with her long blonde hair, had a beauty that shone with the faintest curve of a smile. Everyone knew that Mack was the one who fell deep into the pool of love and thrashed like crazy to hold his head above the water until Ella rescued him.

That was part of family history. How Ella had tamed Mackenzie, replacing his wildness with something much more satisfying, a union of souls.

King's birth had, as each of his parents told him constantly, completed their world. All they'd needed was a small house on an island where the three of them could form a perfect nest of contentment as King grew from toddler to small boy to the man he was becoming.

At King's birth, Ella had suggested they name their son William Mackenzie, a reversal of Mack's name, Mackenzie William. Naturally,

Mack liked the thought of someone in his image but not his clone. Then Ella had pulled a small trick on her adoring and doting husband by suggesting the addition of a second and unique middle name, Lyon. Mack often said the infant's full name of William Lyon Mackenzie King was almost longer than the baby himself.

With Ella's customary sly sense of humor, she didn't ever reveal the reason for suggesting Lyon. No, she waited and fully enjoyed the moment when, years later, someone pointed out a strange coincidence. Just shy of King's ninth birthday, King and Mack finally learned that there had been another William Lyon Mackenzie King. A Canadian, just like his mother Ella. But unlike her, this Canadian was a long-dead prime minister. Ella had found a way to make their family uniquely Canadian while living on the American side of the border.

King, who had looked up photos of the other William Lyon Mackenzie King, had been okay with the Canadian part because he, like everybody, loved Ella. It was the part about sharing the name of an old man with no hair who looked like a bulldog that had no appeal to him.

On the other hand, what was really cool was seeing a movie about King Mufasa and Queen Sarabi and their son Simba. Yes, *The Lion King*. Or *The Lyon King*, the movie in his mind, in which he naturally played a center role.

So about the time he learned he'd been saddled with a name to honor a fusty old politician long put into a grave, King rejected his link to a prime minister by pronouncing himself the Lyon King, and he did it with such consistency that others on the island had given up fighting it.

Life as the Lyon King had been wonderful. He and Mack made no secret that they were the two biggest members of the Ella King fan club, and they kept her on a pedestal, where her bright light filled their home.

Then ten days earlier, while Mack and Ella were in Seattle, Ella collapsed without warning on a sidewalk outside a Starbucks. Physicians still couldn't explain why. All they knew was that nothing could seem to bring her out of a coma. And no one could guess when she might recover. Or if she would.

With her in a coma, the light in King's home had been extinguished. The nest destroyed. No metaphor could come close to describing the misery and dejection Mack and King were enduring while Ella hovered between life and death. And both Mack and the Lyon King were helpless to do anything about it.

※

In a small workshop behind King's house, Ella had a pottery wheel and paints and a kiln. She made coffee cups and bowls and vases and jugs and earned a living selling most of them online. She was proud of her independence, but she insisted on handling all kitchen duty as well because she took joy in taking care of her two men.

But as King walked into the house at supper time, Blake's iPhone in his back pocket, there was no smell of sizzling sausage to greet him. No singing in the kitchen.

The kitchen felt dusty now. King and Mack just made sandwiches whenever they were hungry. Since the coma, they had not sat down once for a meal together. The house was silent because the only thing that mattered, the only thing that was worth discussing, was too painful to mention. The silence was an unbearable reminder that the family had been reduced to the two of them.

Ella also had a thing for cuckoo clocks. Her collection was scattered throughout the house. Little clocks. Big clocks. When the house finally began to sound like a ticking time bomb, Mack had begged Ella to keep only three clocks wound.

But now even the clocks were silent. When Ella entered the coma, King and Mack let the clocks go quiet. They didn't need cheerful reminders on the hour that Ella was not around to enjoy the carved wooden creatures that sprang out.

King needed food. He threw a slice of bread on a plate, slapped some presliced cheese and luncheon meats on it, squirted it with mayo, and covered it with another slice of bread. And yes, he drank milk straight from the carton. He'd always done that when Ella was around, mainly because of her indignant squeal whenever she caught him. Now he drank from the carton because it took less effort than getting a cup from the dirty dishes in the sink and rinsing it.

When Mack walked into the house, King was standing at the sink, staring out the window and thinking about Ella and wondering what criminal act Mack had committed and letting the depression slowly sink down on him as the night slowly fell on the view outside.

"Hey," Mack said to King. "Good to see you back in time for curfew."

Curfew. This echoed in King's mind. *"Trust no authorities. They will hunt you too."* Was that the reason for curfew? Something that Blake had found? That involved Mack?

"Hey," King said in reply without moving. King didn't know if he could keep his face neutral if he turned. He worried that Mack would see that King had betrayed him, that King no longer thought Mack was nearly perfect, that King could no longer trust the father he had once worshipped and adored just as they both worshipped and adored Ella.

King waited for Mack to ask about why King had been kicked out of the homeschool writing class. When nothing came, King wondered if Raimer had decided not to report anything to the warden. That made sense. King had been defiant, but making it an issue would raise a lot of other issues that Raimer might not like.

"Hungry?" Mack said.

"Already ate," King answered. With Ella at the hospital, scheduling decent meals didn't matter much in the King household.

"Good," Mack said.

Just down the road, at their neighbors' house, a dog named Patches began to bark. Patches didn't need a reason to bark. Or if Patches needed a reason, it was beyond any human ability to comprehend. Before Ella had gone into a coma, hearing Patches would prompt King or Mack to make up something, the stupider the better.

"A butterfly must have drifted into Patches' airspace."

"Patches just released some gas and doesn't know it was his."

But now, King and Mack just let the dog bark without comment. None of the old rituals mattered anymore.

Ella was ALONE. Mack wouldn't let King visit.

King smelled wood dust on Mack, even across the space that separated them. It was only the space of the small kitchen, but it felt like opposite sides of the universe. Wood dust. That was Mack's escape. Mack worked the day shift at the prison, and at night, he liked working with wood, making delicate pieces of furniture. His wood shop shared a common wall with Ella's clay room.

King heard the sound of the fridge opening. He knew what Mack would do. Throw bread on a plate, slap presliced cheese and luncheon meat with mayo on the first slice, and add a second slice to hold it in place. The only difference in their routine was that Mack drank his milk from a cup. That's because Mack couldn't take the entire carton back to the wood shop. Which explained the dirty dishes in the sink.

"Tomorrow?" King asked without looking back at his father. He'd only see what never changed. A broad shouldered man with a dark beard filled with wood dust. Square face. Square head. Eyes that could focus like lasers. Except now they seemed dull because of what had happened to Ella.

Mack knew what King was asking about—a chance to go off the island and visit Ella at the hospital.

"Won't work," Mack said. "Maybe a few days from now."

King had only been off the island once since the coma. He'd spent three hours at the hospital, holding Ella's soft hands, whispering to her as he begged her to wake up. After that, Mack had kept both of them prisoners on the island, relying on doctor's reports to see if anything had changed.

"This is unfair, Mack," King said. "I should be able to see her. What if…"

King couldn't finish the sentence. *What if she dies?*

King didn't get a response. He heard his father's footsteps leave the kitchen and knew that, like every other night since Ella had entered the coma, Mack was escaping back to the construction of pieces of furniture.

Until the email from Blake Watt, King had believed that Ella was the entire reason for Mack's withdrawal from family life and any real conversation with King. Now King had no choice but to wonder if it was something different.

"Trust no authorities. They will hunt you too."

CHAPTER 9

"I got nothing," Johnson said. "I thought about it all night. Well, except when I was asleep. But I was thinking about it when I fell asleep. And it was the first thing I thought of when I woke up. And I thought about it all morning. Still nothing. He did not give me the password. Any password."

King and Johnson sat on reclining chairs on the front porch of King's house. The view might have given them a sweep of the open farmland that had been cut into the trees on the island. Except for the drizzle.

The overhang protected them from the moisture, and the breeze wasn't strong enough to blow the drizzle across their faces. The beads of water were so light that it seemed more like fog than light rain, but the gurgling of drain pipes gave proof that the water did not remain suspended in the air.

An empty rocking chair was farther down the porch. This was where Ella would sit on days like this, wrapped in a blanket, hands curled around a tea mug, smile on her face. She loved the coziness and tranquility of this kind of afternoon.

King used to love them too. Until The Coma. Now he hated anything like this that reminded him she was gone. He hated the island.

So he was glad to be frustrated. It took his mind off the empty rocking chair.

"That's impossible," King told Johnson. "Somehow, Watt gave you the password to the iPhone."

"I don't have it," Johnson said.

"He went to a lot of work to set everything up so far. He found a way to beat the infrared sensors in the forbidden zone so he could hide the iPhone and mark the tree. Set up a way to get me a message after he drowned. Made sure the sensors wouldn't detect me either. No way after all of that would he be wrong about you and the password."

"Nothing," Johnson said. "Absolutely, flat-out nothing."

King hit the power button at the top of the iPhone. The home screen lit up, showing the four empty boxes. There were 10,000 possible passwords between 0000 and 9999—except for the two wrong guesses King had put into the phone the day before. Only two chances left. Two more possible passwords to enter before all the data was wiped.

Maybe he should just get it over with. Try two more random passwords. Ensure the data was wiped. Then this whole situation would be out of his hands. He wouldn't be able to do a thing after that to learn whether something crazy and insane bad was happening at night.

But the clock was ticking. All of yesterday, last night, and this morning had passed since he'd found the iPhone. Easily half of the 72-hour deadline that Watt's email had threatened until a new set of emails went out into the world to show that King's father was a horrible criminal involved in a crazy and insane bad thing that was supposedly happening at night.

King wanted to think the key word was "supposedly." However, the argument that he'd just used on Johnson was too powerful. No way Watt would have set all of this up if something wasn't happening. For crying out loud, there was the simple fact that Watt had been worried enough to put in a dead man's switch. And then the horrible truth that Watt's worries had come true when he drowned.

Something *was* happening. And King needed Johnson to come up with more than just "I got nothing."

"He must have given you some kind of clue," King said. "Maybe he didn't come out and say, 'Hey, buddy, remember this password in case I die.' But can't you remember anything that seemed unusual enough to point to a password?"

"I got nothing," Johnson said.

"Getting a little tired of hearing that," King said. "Did he ever give you anything? Anything at all?"

Johnson shrugged. "A flashlight that didn't work."

King stood. He walked to one of the support beams of the porch and pretended to bang his head against it a few times. He sat.

"What?" Johnson said.

"Here's how it works," King said. "Something out of the ordinary like that. The first thing you do when I ask you about Blake is go, 'A flashlight that doesn't work.' Maybe it means something."

"Give me a break. I just remembered it now. When you asked. Just now. Before, you were just talking about passwords."

"A flashlight that doesn't work. That doesn't seem significant?"

"Not when you ask about passwords."

"He didn't say anything else when he gave it to you?"

Johnson's eyes began to widen.

"Yeah," King said. "He did say something."

"I don't want to tell you," Johnson said. "You'll get mad at me because now that I think about it…"

"I won't get mad. I promise."

"He gave it to me and told me to hang on to it. He said he wanted me to hide it for him and if I didn't tell anyone about it, he'd give me a hundred bucks someday to give it back to him."

King took a deep breath. "I won't get mad…if you tell me that you still have it."

"Of course I do," Johnson said. "I forgot about it until now."

King took another deep breath. "And?"

"I put it between my mattress and box spring."

CHAPTER 10

In the hallway, Johnson told King, "Don't say anything about my bedroom, okay?"

"Sure."

"Seriously, not a word."

King could have walked blindfolded through Johnson's house and led them to every room. The layout of the small farmhouse was identical to King's house, which was identical to half of the houses that had been built for employee families decades earlier.

It wasn't decorated the same, of course. Especially Johnson's room.

"Um…" King said. "Elvis?"

"You said you wouldn't say a word," Johnson said.

"That was until I saw Elvis. How can you not say something at a poster like that?"

Elvis was on a huge poster. He wore a white jumpsuit, looking as if he was screaming as he held a microphone close. Psychedelic colors filled the background.

"Star Wars," King said, looking at another poster. "That makes a little more sense. Not much more, but a little more." He turned to another poster. "And—"

"Enough," Johnson cut him off before King could say "dragon."

"But—"

"Enough! Shut the door and hit the light switch."

King followed instructions. The room went dark. That's when he realized that Johnson had dark towels across the windows to keep out daylight. What was weird was how the posters glowed in the dark.

Johnson was wearing a black shirt, and dust specks seemed to glow on the shirt.

"Black light," Johnson said. "My bulbs are black light. They give out ultraviolet light. Those are vintage posters. Specially made to glow in the black light. I collect some and buy and sell others on eBay."

"You never told me about this."

"So that you could mock me about Elvis? I wonder why not. Collectors get serious about this kind of stuff. I knew you wouldn't understand. You're too cool. You're the Lyon King."

King opened the door and light flooded in, diminishing the glow on the posters. He snapped off the lights and the glow faded completely.

"So you make money buying and selling this," King said. "That's impressive."

"Nice try. I know when you're trying to be nice. I've watched you do it to others for years."

Johnson went to his bed. Neatly made. The bed covers were so tight that King understood what it meant to talk about bouncing quarters off a bed. Everything about Johnson's room was neat.

Johnson reached under and pulled out the flashlight. He flicked it on. "See, nothing."

King had a flash of intuition. "Did Blake know about these posters?"

"Yeah," Johnson said. "He was a geek too. A different kind of geek. But I knew he wouldn't laugh. And he didn't."

"So maybe it's a black-light flashlight," King said. He closed the door and did not snap on the bedroom lights. "Try it now."

In the darkness, nothing happened.

"Try it now," King repeated.

"I did," Johnson said. "Obviously nothing is happening."

King opened the bedroom door again. "Can I see the flashlight?"

Johnson handed it to him. King unscrewed it. "Maybe the batteries are dead."

He pulled out the batteries. There was a small wad of paper between them. "Interesting," King said. "This would have prevented a connection."

He noticed writing on the paper. All it said was "The Room."

"The Room," King repeated. "Remember, that was one of the hints for you."

"And remember I said I didn't know what room Blake was talking about?" Johnson answered.

King put the batteries back in and screwed the flashlight back together. He flicked on the switch and closed the bedroom door. The posters began to glow.

"Bingo," King said. "A flashlight with an ultraviolet bulb."

"You can get them easy on the Internet," Johnson said. "Just like I ordered the special bulbs for my bedroom."

King open the door again so he could look at the flashlight in the daylight. Maybe it had some other clues.

"Um…" Johnson said.

"Um?"

"The Room. I'm kind of remembering something."

King fought the impulse to sigh. Johnson could drive him nuts sometimes. But on the other hand, just yesterday Johnson had stood beside King in the classroom fight against Raimer, and for Johnson, that had taken a lot of courage. You take the good with the bad, King thought.

"The Room," Johnson repeated. "Both words capitalized. It's a cool game app. In the game, there's a special light you use to shine on objects to see if there are invisible words hidden on them. Invisible words that give clues. Maybe on the iPhone…"

King shut the bedroom door again. He could hear Johnson's breath close beside him in the near-total dark. King pulled Blake's iPhone out of his own pocket. He flicked on the flashlight again. The front of the iPhone was glass. There would be little chance of anything on the glass.

King shone the ultraviolet light on the black metal backing of the iPhone.

Four numbers glowed at them: 2855.

CHAPTER 11

"Wow," Johnson said, squinting at the screen of the iPhone. "All those folders. You said over 3500 games and apps. Can you count that high?"

They weren't near Johnson's house anymore. Holding Blake Watt's iPhone felt like holding a used radioactive core. King had insisted they find some privacy before entering the password. Last thing he wanted was Johnson's mom catching them with it.

So despite the urgency he felt as the hours counted down until the threatened release of whatever secret Blake Watt had felt important enough to hide with a dead man's switch, King and Johnson had strolled—yes, strolled so that anyone watching would think they were wandering around the way kids do—back to the shoreline that gave them a view across the sound. The same place where King had asked Johnson the day before about the chances of swimming off the island.

They found shade beneath some spruce near the water, and the quiet slap of small waves on the pebbled shore concealed their whispered conversation.

King had put in the password: 2855.

And the screen had given them access. The home page had a grid of 20 folders. Five vertical and four horizontal. Blake had filled each folder with 16 apps.

King had thumbed through the pages. Eleven home pages, each filled with 20 folders.

"Don't need to count," King said. "There's this amazing invention called math. Eleven times 20 times 16."

"Hate math," Johnson said. "Math is like from the Middle Ages. The more amazing invention is called a calculator."

"Which the iPhone has, right?"

King brought up a search bar. He typed "calc," which brought up Calculator. King tapped on the app, and when it opened, he plugged in the numbers. Eleven times 20 times 16. The total was 3520. That's how many games or apps were on the black iPhone 5. King knew that Blake had jailbroken the iPhone, but he didn't know if that was the limit set by Apple or if Blake had tweaked it. Either way, that was a crazy amount of apps and games.

"He was a serious geek," Johnson said.

"I don't think he did anything by accident," King answered. "That should be obvious by now. So that means we need to ask ourselves if there is a reason for so many apps."

"Distraction?" Johnson said. "I mean, isn't this about an email? Or emails?"

In answer, King tapped the mail icon at the bottom of the iPhone. The mail opened and showed zero emails in the inbox.

"Wait for it…" King said, watching the spinning gray tics that showed the mail program was searching for emails. "Wait for it…"

The signal strength bars at the top of the iPhone showed excellent coverage. ATT.

The phone gave a pleasant sound. Email received and downloaded.

With Johnson watching, King tapped on the email.

It opened. And…

…nothing.

"Huh?" Johnson said.

"Huh is right," King said. "It's a blank message. And look at the header. The From and To."

The headers matched. From: blakewatt2855@gmail.com. To: blakewatt2855@gmail.com.

"Blake sending something to Blake?" Johnson said.

King didn't answer. He was thinking.

"No," Johnson said. "It could be a message from Blake. He told us he wasn't going to send you anything anymore in case it could be traced from his account. So he set up a different account. Used numbers instead of a name."

"But why send a blank message?" King tapped his front tooth. Maybe all of this was a sick joke. After all, Mack really couldn't be behind anything crazy and insane and bad happening at night.

"I got it," Johnson said. "Invisible ink."

"Sure," King answered. "Like on the back of the phone. You're saying we just use the magic flashlight, and it will show up on here?"

"Yeah. Er, no. You can't use a marker on an email. I need to stop getting so excited and use my brain before I talk."

King was tapping his tooth again.

"Actually," King said. "You may be right. Blake once played a trick on me. I think he did it again. Come on. We need to go back to your house and make sure the coast is clear."

CHAPTER 12

"Doily?" King snorted. A wide circular hand-knitted flower sat beneath the computer monitor. "A doily?"

They were back at Johnson's house. In a nook just off the kitchen, a computer workstation had been built into a corner. On the wall behind it was a bulletin board with coupons pinned on one side and family photos on the other.

The nook smelled of fresh lemon. Artificial fresh lemon. Johnson's mom was a freak about using furniture polish. Dust was instantly eliminated from the Johnson home. It made King sad, worrying about whether Ella would ever return to their own house. To wind the cuckoo clocks. To stand at the stove, stirring macaroni as the water boiled, fresh clay stuck to the cuticles of her nails from her time at the spinning wheel.

"Think of it as an ornamental mat," Johnson sighed. "Meant to protect the desktop." He sighed again. "And if it matters, the name comes from Doiley, a draper in London who popularized them in the 1600s."

"And you know this how?" King forced away his sadness.

"You know it's called a doily. Most kids wouldn't."

"But this draper stuff…"

"I told my mom that whatever she had knitted to put under the monitor probably wouldn't be a hot accessory at the Apple store. That's when she forced me to Google it with her and learn the history. I think she was trying to teach me not to mock her sense of fashion. It worked."

"Doily," King said again. "We're using a monitor on a doily to bust a set of mysteries from a computer geek."

"That's perfect," Johnson said. "After all, who would think to go to this computer?"

"Only if my theory is right," King answered.

Johnson looked around, obviously nervous about getting caught. "Let's be fast, okay? I don't know how long we have until Mom gets back. She's not in good shape, and when she goes for a run, it's never that far."

"I locked the door as we came in," King said.

Johnson groaned. "And if I don't see her in time, I would explain that how? We don't have to lock doors on the island."

Maybe now, King thought. *"Trust no authorities. They will hunt you too."* He didn't say it though. "Your mother. Your problem."

"One thing," Johnson said. "I won't lie. Just so you understand. If we get busted, I won't lie. I'll tell them about the iPhone. I mean, it's killing me to hide it. We should have never bought it for Blake. We should have never—"

"The door," King said. "Listen. Did someone try to open it?"

Johnson snapped his mouth shut and strained to hear.

"That's better," King said. "Silence."

"Ha, ha. Come on. Get going."

King unlocked the phone again with 2855.

"Here's what I'm thinking," King said. "Blake—if this really was Blake who set up the emails—was paranoid that somebody could track emails sent to me via my server. So he just sent the one original email and told me to trash it. Even if someone found that first email, they wouldn't get the rest of the trail. That's why he's now using this iPhone to get us the rest of his emails. Anyone trying to trace his original stuff won't know this new email account or that we have access to it."

"With you so far. But he only sent us one email. Blank."

"I want to forward that email to a computer that's not mine or yours." King thumbed on the keypad, putting in Johnson's mom's email address. "Then we read it and trash it. I can't believe we need to be this paranoid, but I guess it won't hurt."

"Unless my mom walks in and asks why we're at her computer instead of mine."

"Locked door."

"Which, as I thought I made clear, is going to be awkward to explain if—"

"Listen," King said, holding up a hand. There it was—the woosh of an email sent by iPhone.

Almost instantly, the computer in front of them pinged. One new message.

"Open it," King told Johnson.

"I shouldn't be in her emails," Johnson said. "I hate this."

"Not as much as you'd hate the world learning something about this island that makes our dads look like criminals."

King wasn't feeling so bad about this lie to Johnson. Is that what happened to people? You just got used to doing wrong things? Is that how Mack was led to whatever crime Blake had found?

"Doing this means we half believe it's true," Johnson said. "I hate that too. It's like we're betraying our dads."

Johnson had read King's thoughts. "Yeah. I'm with you on that. So don't think about it. Open the email."

King tried not to think about how he was lying to Johnson about this. Johnson's dad wasn't involved. Only King's dad. So King was betraying his dad and his best friend. But what choice did he have?

Johnson clicked on the email King had forwarded from the iPhone. As expected, the content of the email was blank. Just as it had been on the iPhone.

"Click on the contents," King said. "Command-A."

"Select all?"

"That's a rhetorical question, right?" King said.

"Like yours," Johnson said. He clicked on the keyboard.

"Now bring up font styles," King said.

Johnson did.

King pointed at the monitor. "Ha!"

"Ha?"

"The font is white," King said. "Sometimes you use a white font against a colored background. But against a white background…"

Johnson whistled. "Like invisible ink."

Without waiting for King to say anything, Johnson selected black for font color. Words popped up on the screen.

"Bingo," King said.

"No, trouble," Johnson said. He glanced over King's shoulder and out the window, and his eyes widened. "Here comes my mom back from her jog."

"Print it," King said, tucking the iPhone in his back pocket. Calm on the outside, feeling not so calm interior. "I'll get the door."

King took a step then stopped. "And delete the email!"

King reached the door and unlocked it a full second before Johnson's mom turned the knob. He had just enough time to get back to a chair and pretend he was relaxing.

She opened the door. White cords dangled from her earbuds. Her face was flushed, her brown hair curled and wet at the edges. She was wearing a plain gray jogging suit.

King waved.

She pulled the earbuds loose.

"Hello, Mrs. Johnson," King felt the iPhone in his back pocket pressing against him, a reminder of all his deceit, beginning with buying the device for Blake Watt. "I hope you're okay that I was thinking of raiding your cookie jar."

She smiled. "For the Lyon King? Sure."

It had never occurred to King before, but Lyon King sure sounded a lot like Lying King.

CHAPTER 13

"This really is insane," Johnson told King as they stepped onto a small pier. McNeil Island had a reservoir in the center of it, shaped like a wedge of pie. It had been stocked with trout, and catch-and-release fishing was permitted. There were some monstrous fish.

"Extremely insane," King said. "But isn't there a part of you that's having fun?"

Sun threw their shadows in front of them as they walked on the creaky weathered wood. Each carried fishing rods and small tackle boxes. The printed email Blake had sent told them to go fishing. And to keep the flashlight in the tackle box.

"Now what?" Johnson said. King noticed that Johnson didn't answer the question about whether this was fun.

"Well, this is the only place Blake ever went fishing with us. Once."

"And squealed like a little girl when you told him he had to thread a worm on the hook. Remember? It freaked him out so bad he threw the worm as far as he could. Then he just watched us fish."

"He learned the squealing part from you," King said.

"It happens." Johnson shrugged. "At least I was a good teacher."

"I think that's the point," King answered. "He set up a trail that only we can follow. If—and I'm just saying *if*—people really are trying to spy on our emails and learn what he's telling us, there's no way these clues would mean anything to them. I was able to figure out his invisible ink in the email because he had once played that joke on me. And if someone else had actually intercepted that email and then figured out the white font on the white background, how would they know exactly where to go fishing? Blake only went once with us. Here."

"He was a little girl," Johnson sniffed. Johnson flexed a pitiful bicep. "Not manly like me."

"You do know what the word 'delusional' means, right?"

"Sure I do—" Johnson stopped. "Hey, were you just calling me—"

"Yes, Sherlock."

They'd reached the end of the dock. Where all three of them had sat on the one afternoon that Blake Watt went fishing with them. "Check it out."

A tiny arrow had been scratched into the wood. It pointed at the opposite side of the lake.

"Something is waiting for us at the other side?" Johnson said.

"Hmm." King realized he was tapping his front tooth again. He stopped himself. It was like sending out a signal to other people. As a rule, he didn't like showing others how he was feeling. In this case, of course, he felt puzzled.

"How far across," King said. "A half mile?"

"Maybe."

"If the arrow was pointing across the lake and it was off by a couple of degrees, do you have any idea how much you could miss the target by?"

"Nope," Johnson said in the tone of voice that indicated he wasn't going to strain his brain.

"Think of it like you were standing here with a rifle and tried to shoot at an empty can half a mile away. You might miss by ten yards, even if there was only a slight wobble when you pulled the trigger. And that's using a barrel a couple feet long to line up with a target. This arrow in the wood is only about an inch long. No way could Blake have meant that we needed to use it to align with something far away."

King dropped to his stomach and peered over the edge.

"Never gets old being right," he grunted.

He pushed himself up again. "There's another line scratched into the wood. Vertical. The arrow up here points at that vertical line. So whatever we're looking for is straight down."

"The water is ten feet deep here. And the note told us to go fishing, not diving."

King was already getting his fishing rod ready. A small lead weight was crimped to the end of the line. About four feet above the weight, a hook was attached to the main line with a shorter piece of line. And above that, a bobber. The method was to put a worm on the hook and let the lead weight take the line down so that the worm and the hook floated a couple feet above the lead weight. The plastic bobber—about the size of a golf ball—floated on the surface. If a trout took the bait, the movement of the bobber would show it.

King dropped the hook down without baiting it.

He made wide arcs back and forth.

"We're doing what?" Johnson asked.

"Sweeping," King said. "Trying to snag whatever he has floating down there for us to find."

"Does it get old being wrong?" Johnson asked. "Blake didn't go to all this work just so someone who really went fishing here would find it by accident. We're not the only ones to use this dock."

"All right, wise guy," King said. "What's your suggestion?"

"Hand me your fishing rod."

King did.

Johnson shoved King off the end of the dock.

King came up sputtering and indignant. He treaded water facing the end of the dock. "That's your idea? Shoving me into the water?"

"Only part of it," Johnson said. "From where you are, take a closer look at the line scratched into the wood."

"Death shall be thy reward," King said. "You're lucky the iPhone isn't in my back pocket." King had hidden it in the woods.

"I thought of that," Johnson said. "Really. Now tell me if the scratched line continues. You know, like maybe something is hidden under the pier.

King wasn't going to admit the water felt good. Or that Johnson had actually come up with a good idea.

King peered at the vertical line. He noticed it continued to the bottom of the wood as if the scratched line was wrapping around and continuing.

Was there something on the back of the strip of wood at the end of the pier?

King paddled closer. He reached behind. His fingers touched something cool and smooth. It swayed.

Swayed?

King swam beneath the pier and looked up. The sunlight was striped, knifing through the gaps between the crossbeams of the pier.

"Hey!"

There was Johnson, directly above. The wood creaked as Johnson shifted weight.

King ignored his friend. Hanging from a nail, at the end of a piece of fishing line, was a short, wide piece of metal. That's why it had swayed. Like a pendulum.

King clutched it and ducked into the water again to come out at the end of pier.

Johnson squinted at him.

"Something," King said. Still treading water, he held up the piece of metal. It was a dull gunmetal gray.

"Never gets old," Johnson said. "Being right."

"Take it." King reached up. "Put it in the tackle box so it's safe."

King didn't say the rest. *Not only safe, but hidden.*

Johnson was careful. He took it in both hands.

"Interesting," Johnson said as King pulled himself onto the dock.

"What?"

Johnson lifted the piece of metal from the tackle box. Four fishing hooks clung to it.

"Unless I'm delusional, it's a magnet," Johnson said. "A strong magnet. Those fishing hooks jumped right on it. Why would Blake give us a magnet?"

CHAPTER 14

"Got something!" Mike squealed like a little girl and raised the tip of his rod. He always sounded like this when he hooked a fish. Except this time, it wasn't a fish.

"No you don't," King answered. "Keep the rod down."

They were sitting now, both of them at the edge of the pier, bare feet dangling in the water. Both sets of shoes were on the dock behind them.

"I'm telling you," Mike said, "your theory was right."

It had been a simple theory. King had guessed the arrow scratched in the wood pointed not only to the magnet hidden under the dock but also to the purpose of the magnet. King had guessed that somewhere below was something for the magnet to catch.

So King had replaced the lead weight at the end of his fishing line with the magnet, and Mike had started sweeping the magnet along the bottom.

"And I'm telling you," King said, "that Murdoch just drove out of the woods and turned onto the dirt road and is headed this way. Look now, but don't make it obvious. And leave your line in the water."

Over their right shoulders, on a small road that led from the trees to the reservoir, a gleaming black Jeep TJ with an open top and shiny mag wheels headed toward the dock. Only one person drove that Jeep on the island because that one person wanted to keep it that way, and he had unquestioned authority on the island.

Warden Murdoch was a tall man, and his body swayed slightly to the bouncing of the Jeep. Wind had been blowing away from King and MJ, and the noise of the Jeep finally reached them as it covered the last 200 yards to the edge of the water.

From the Jeep, Murdoch smiled and waved. He dressed like a cowboy who liked his Stetson. It was common knowledge on the island that when he wanted to be the boss—to give orders or chew someone out—he wore the hat. So if he walked toward you wearing the Stetson, he was doing it to look even taller than he was and wanted to intimidate you. But if he wasn't wearing the Stetson, he was in a good mood or just wanted to pretend to be one of the guys.

He was wearing the hat behind the steering wheel.

Not good, King thought.

But when Murdoch stepped out of the Jeep, he removed it and set it on the passenger seat.

Still not good, King thought.

He and Johnson had a magnet at the end of a fishing line, and if Johnson was correct, something was on the end of the magnet, and if King was correct, that something had been planted there by Blake Watt, and if Blake Watt was correct, King and Johnson should be worried about the message that said TRUST NO AUTHORITIES because the most authoritative of authorities on the island was headed their way.

The dock creaked as Warden Murdoch placed his weight on the first boards. Murdoch's hair was slicked back. He wore a suit that King had heard cost $2000. He also wore shiny cowboy boots that were rumored to be as expensive as his suit. The bolo necktie—a cord with decorative metal tips and an ornamental clasp—that was supposed to be cowboy cool had some kind of polished Navajo blue turquoise set in polished silver.

King winced at the thought of Johnson pushing Murdoch into the water. Both of them would probably be thrown into a cell deep in the prison and never be seen again. Murdoch was known not only for spending money on how he looked but also for losing it big time when he got mad.

"Nice day for fishing?" Murdoch called out. He was good cop today. Other days, bad cop.

"Nice day for sitting in the sun," King said.

Murdoch reached them.

"Also a nice day to get outsmarted by fish," King said to Murdoch. King elbowed Johnson. "Show him the hook."

MJ's face went a shade white, but he caught on quickly. He raised the rod high enough to show the empty hook tied into the line about four feet above where King usually had a lead weight. MJ left the bottom part of the line in the water. King was glad the water wasn't too clear. The magnet at the end of the line and whatever it might be holding remained out of sight.

King took the rod from Johnson. He slid the rod under his elbow to bring the empty hook in closer without lifting the magnet any higher.

"Hand me a worm," he said to Johnson. It seemed important to really sell Murdoch on the fact that King and Johnson were actually fishing. To Murdoch, King said. "MJ hates worm guts. I always have to do this part for him."

Johnson dug into the tackle box for a jar with bait. King had prepared for the one-in-a-hundred chance that someone might show up while they were on the dock, and taking along live worms had been part of it. Never got old, being right.

"Wanted to talk to you guys about Blake Watt," Murdoch said. He remained standing, throwing both of them into a shadow.

King held a worm that wriggled uselessly in the air. He jabbed the point of a hook in it and pushed the worm along the metal of the hook. He dropped the line back in the water and kept possession of the rod.

"Did someone…um, find the body?" MJ asked.

At the funeral, the casket had been empty. King and Johnson both knew that Blake's parents were holding out hope that Blake had not drowned, but instead managed to survive the frigid water that no one else had ever survived, cross the dangerous currents of the sound, and run away. It was a terrible thing when parents could only cling to a hope that their son was wandering homeless in the streets of a city somewhere.

"No," Murdoch said. "I'm just wondering if either of you knew anything about Blake ever having access to the Internet. I thought maybe you'd speak honestly to me in case you had been afraid to tell his parents anything when they were on the island. Now that they're gone, I promise if you help me with this, no one else will know."

"Sir?" King asked, instead of directly lying.

Murdoch sighed. "What I'm going to talk to you guys about is strictly between the three of us. It's unkind to speak ill of the dead."

CHAPTER 15

"Blake wasn't supposed to get Internet access for the same reason his parents moved to the island," Murdoch began. "Back in Lincoln, Nebraska, Blake's mom was a successful bank executive. His father was a psychology professor. Blake developed computer skills early. When he was 11, he hacked into computers at the university. He could go in and change students' grades if he wanted. Six months ago, he hacked into the computers at his mom's bank. He said he was doing it to protect the bank—to prove that if he could get into it, someone else could. It would have been a good argument, but he transferred some money from a big account to an account he owned. So his father applied for a position here at the prison to isolate Blake."

King tried to keep his face neutral. He hoped Johnson could do the same. Together, they had given Blake Internet access. And Blake had stolen money from his mom's bank? Hard to imagine what Blake might have done on the island after King and Johnson got him the phone. This alone could put Murdoch into a bad cop screaming fit. And then there was the rest of it, which had led to King and MJ sitting here with a fishing rod and a magnet at the end of the line.

"Anyway," Murdoch said, "weird things have happened at some of the prison computers. Like someone has maybe planted a virus. I don't know much about computers, and I think I'm going to need to bring someone in from off the island to look at it. I wanted to check with you guys first to see if you think Blake could have had anything to do with it."

"Wish I could help," King said. "Blake didn't talk much about any computer stuff."

This was true...at least when Blake was alive. Blake was saying plenty now with emails from the dead.

"Got nothing," Johnson said. "Sorry sir."

"Got nothing is bad grammar," Murdoch said. "And son, I have to say that bad grammar irritates me. What's next, walking around with your pants half down so that the entire world sees your undershorts?"

That's when something struck the worm on the line in the water. The tip of the rod dipped abruptly.

Without thinking, King gave the rod a quick yank to set the hook. He'd done it so many times, the reflex had become second nature.

King immediately regretted his instinctive move. The last thing he wanted at this moment was a fish on the line.

Too late.

The tip of the rod moved in small circles, and where the line went into the water, larger circles cut through the surface.

The fish was securely hooked.

But it couldn't make much of a run. There was too much weight at the end of the line, four feet below the hook. A heavy magnet and whatever might be stuck to it.

"Don't be slow," Murdoch said. "Let's see what you have."

King would have been okay if he lost the fish. He *wouldn't* have been okay if the line snapped. Then either the fish would be stuck to a magnet until it died, or if it was big enough, the fish would drag the magnet and whatever it held out into the middle of the reservoir.

By the way the end of the rod was bent, this was not a small fish.

King could feel the fish try to move toward the dock. Maybe looking to wrap the line around one of the supporting posts. That told King the fish was big enough to be smart enough.

He reeled hard, and the back of the fish broke the surface of the water as it flapped.

Johnson rescued them. He'd already taken the fishing net and scooped it into the water beneath the fish.

With King lifting the rod higher and Johnson taking the weight of the fish with the net, they brought the fish in. Out of the water, they could see it was a trout. If King had to guess, he'd say four pounds. Big for a trout.

Guessing the weight correctly, however was not King's biggest concern. He was much more focused on keeping the magnet hidden. With Johnson holding the net out of the water, King still needed to keep the rod low enough so the magnet remained beneath the surface.

Johnson handed King the net, so King had the rod in one hand and the net in the other. Now King's task was easier to accomplish.

He was impressed that Johnson stayed cool. He'd never seen this side of MJ before. After all, the warden had just asked about Blake and Internet access, and if the warden knew about the magnet, all the warden had to do was reach down for proof about Blake—and the questions this would lead to were terrifying.

"Trust no authorities. They will hunt you too."

Johnson leaned forward and dipped his hands into the water so they wouldn't feel like sandpaper on the fish's skin. With water dripping from his fingertips, Johnson managed to hold the fish securely with both hands.

"Sir," Johnson said, still cool. "Mind grabbing a pair of pliers from the tackle box?"

Again, King congratulated himself on leaving Blake's iPhone hidden behind them in the woods. Otherwise, it would have been right there for Murdoch to see.

Murdoch squatted between King and Johnson, and King caught the smell of the man's cologne. He also caught himself noticing that it was a nice smell, not too heavy but not too girlie. A strange thought to have as King was desperately trying to keep the magnet hidden beneath the water.

"Flashlight?" Murdoch said as he opened the toolbox. "You guys fish at night? You know that spotlighting fish is illegal, right?"

Murdoch snapped the switch on and checked the bulb. "Dead. Guess that gets you two off the hook." Murdoch laughed at his own joke.

"Sir?" Johnson said. "Pliers? Hate to hurt this fish more than it is."

Murdoch grabbed the pliers and leaned forward.

King felt his blood curdle. The magnet was dimly visible from this angle. If Murdoch…

The trout turned out to be enough of a distraction. Murdoch focused on the fish, and without getting his own fingers dirty by touching the fish, he used the pliers to work the barbless hook loose from the trout.

"Nice catch," Murdoch said, leaning back. "Supper?"

King lowered the tip of the rod, and the outline of the magnet disappeared.

"No sir," Johnson said. "Catch and release."

"You never break the rules?" Murdoch asked.

King wondered if Murdoch was playing them.

"No sir. King and I, we're good guys. We like freedom."

Johnson didn't drop the trout in the water. It was already facing possible shock from a hook in the mouth and its time in the air. Instead, Johnson leaned down again and held the trout just under the surface until it was obviously stable. Johnson let go, and the trout twisted once and disappeared in a flash.

"How about another worm?" King asked. He was going to match Johnson for cool in this situation.

The warden stood.

"Well, guys," Murdoch said. "Obviously you have better things to do than listen to me. Remember I asked you to keep this secret, and if you learn anything about Blake and computers, be sure to let me know."

CHAPTER 16

The sadness hadn't diminished for King, stepping into a house where his mother no longer lived. It was a constant reminder that across the frigid waters of Puget Sound, she was hooked up to bags that dripped fluids into her veins. She was just a shell. ALONE.

Not the mother who baked muffins and sang and made pottery. Just a shell. ALONE. Why wouldn't Mack let King go to the mainland and sit with Ella? The image of her all alone hit King dozens of times a day, and each time, it drew anger and despair and frustration.

This stuff from Blake would have been a great distraction except for what it could mean about Mack.

Johnson said nothing as they stepped into the empty house. He pretended it was normal even though this was the first time King had invited Johnson into the house since Ella's stroke.

They didn't want to be in Johnson's house. Might lead to questions. So they'd settled on King's. Needing darkness.

Straight to King's bedroom. No mention of Ella and the huge hole that her absence made in the fabric of King's life.

"Should try making the bed someday," Johnson said. It was a swirl of blankets and sheets. "If my dad saw that, he'd freak out. He's on me for every little thing."

"Nobody in this house cares," King said. Enough of an explanation.

King stepped to the window and pulled the drapes. He knew it would be dark enough, even midafternoon. This was, after all, his bedroom. Too many times in the past ten days, he'd lain there in the darkness, wondering about the shell of his mother, her breath in and out, regular, sucked into the coma as if she'd stepped into quicksand. Like quicksand, it was something you didn't see until it was too late. Just like that. A stroke.

"We're assuming Blake wants us to find the answers," King said. "How good is it going to feel to be right again."

Johnson held the flashlight. "No new emails. This has got to be it."

No new emails. After leaving the dock, King had retrieved Blake's iPhone and checked.

"Lights off then," King said, holding the small box that the magnet had snagged from the bottom of the reservoir. This small metallic box had a combination lock. He snapped off the light switch.

And there it was, on the top of the black box. Four numbers. Two. One. Five. Four.

"See it?" King asked.

"Two one five four."

King stepped over to the wall and flipped on the light switch again. The numbers were invisible on the box.

He rotated the numbers into position.

The lid popped.

"Never gets old," Johnson said with a hint of triumph in his voice. "Being—"

What stopped him was the sight of the contents.

Johnson sighed. "Now what?"

The contents of the box consisted of a remote control in a ziplock bag that was in another ziplock bag that was in another ziplock bag. Completely waterproof.

"Blake does want us to get to the end," King said. "We agreed on that, right? And we're the only ones with his flashlight."

King snapped off the bedroom light again. "See if there's anything else."

And there was. On the bottom of the metal box. Glowing white in the ultraviolet light.

ASK SAM TO SHOW YOU HER MEASLES.

CHAPTER 17

"Sam," King asked. "Are you feeling okay?"

King, Johnson, and Samantha were in Sam's neatly mowed front yard. Tips of branches on the large tree centered in the lawn bobbed in a breeze. Samantha sat on a tire hanging from a rope tied to one of the thicker branches higher up. She had a stuffed dog in her lap, big enough that the top of the dog's head touched the bottom of her chin. The dog had a collar with a small pink round disc hanging from the center to match the pink ribbon tied in a bow on its head.

"Great," Samantha said. "I'm feeling great."

"So you don't have measles?" Johnson asked her.

"Yes," she said. Giggled. "I do."

"Measles gives you spots," Johnson said, frowning as he looked at her face. "I don't see anything."

"Yes, you do."

"No, I don't."

"Yes."

"No."

"Yes."

"No."

"Yes."

"Guys," King pleaded, staring at the stuffed dog. He'd seen a picture of it somewhere.

"No," Johnson said, betraying some irritation. "I'm not wrong about this. I don't see anything."

"You got your eyes open." Samantha raised her hands around the stuffed dog. "How many fingers am I holding up?"

"Yeah, yeah," Johnson said. "Okay. I can see."

"How many?" Samantha asked.

King guessed that Samantha enjoyed having someone around and wanted to prolong the conversation just so she wouldn't have to swing on a tire with only a stuffed dog for company. King understood the feeling. The island was lonely.

"We're supposed to see your measles," King said to Samantha. He felt a sense of urgency. "Can you help us?"

"Not until MJ tells me how many fingers I'm holding up. Because I was right—he *can* see."

"A bunch of them," Johnson said. Impatient.

"I'm not talking until you answer right," she said. She emphasized it by pressing her lips tight and blowing her cheeks out. She pressed her chin down on the stuffed dog's head.

"We don't have time for this," Johnson said. "Come on."

Sam shook her head from side to side, and her hair flew straight out.

"Nine," Johnson said.

She continued to shake her head, holding out her fingers for him to count.

"Nine," Johnson said. "I can see and I can count."

Samantha broke her silence to giggle. "Count again."

"Can I answer?" King asked.

"Nope. Just MJ."

"Aaarg," MJ said.

"Multiplication tables," King told him.

"Huh? Multipli—" Johnson stopped himself. "Oh, got it."

He made a show of studying Samantha's fingers. "The pinky is up, the next finger is down, and the rest are up. One and eight. You have 18 fingers up."

Samantha giggled and shook her head again.

"From her perspective," King said. "You can do this, MJ."

Johnson frowned. He held out his own fingers. Took a second to figure it out. "Okay, 81. You have 81 fingers up."

Samantha, with her arms still reached around the stuffed dog, applauded.

"But I don't see measles," Johnson said. He turned to King. "Why can't anything be easy about this?"

"What's supposed to be easy?" Samantha asked.

"MJ," King said. "How about ix-nay on-ay e-they iscussion-day ere-hey?"

"What?" he said.

"Nix on the discussion here," Samantha said. She looked at King. "Whatever you guys are doing, maybe I should help. MJ's not that swift."

"We're good," King said, thinking maybe Samantha had a point.

"So what *aren't* you supposed to be discussing in front of me?" Sam asked.

"Nothing," Johnson said. "Especially with a smart-mouth little girl."

She crossed her arms. "You shouldn't lie to little girls. You wouldn't be here unless you wanted to talk about something. Because you never come over to play. But if you want to discuss nothing, I can do that too."

"MJ," King said, "would you mind getting on your knees and begging forgiveness for calling her a smart-mouth little girl?"

"You sound serious."

"I *am* serious. She's smart, but not a smart-mouth."

"Little too," Sam said. "I'm okay with smart and little."

Johnson knelt.

"Good enough," Sam said before Johnson could speak. "Now tell me how I have Measles."

King liked Samantha and her exhibition of total control of the situation.

"Give us a hint," King said.

She shook her head.

"Remember, I was the one who suggested that MJ kneel like a knight before a princess."

"Okay then. Blake gave me Measles."

"Blake was sick too?" Johnson asked.

King had a hunch. "Sam, how do you spell 'measles'?"

She grinned. "Capital M-e-e-z-elz."

"She's wrong," Johnson said. Triumphant to be smarter than a little girl. "Elz isn't even a letter. It's m-e-a-s-l-e-s."

"Nice," King said. "You won a spelling bee against someone younger than half your age. And by the way, you missed the important part. The capital *M*."

"It's M-e-a?" Sam turned to King, who was obviously the default arbitrator. "Not M-e-e?"

"I like the way you spelled it," King said. "Especially because it had a capital *M*. The one that MJ missed."

"This conversation makes me feel like I'm with Alice in Wonderland," Johnson said. "Really."

"Yeah?" King told him. "I'm the one who had to stop you in the middle of a yes-no argument with a little girl. You'd probably still be in the middle of it."

"No," Johnson said.

"Yes," Samantha said.

"No," Johnson said.

"Yes."

"No."

"MJ!" It came out a little sharper than King intended. But still. Johnson couldn't even figure out that Sam was messing with him.

Johnson looked hurt.

Samantha giggled.

"Sam," King said. "Would it be okay if I held Measles?"

"Sure," Sam said. "Blake said I could have this if I promised I wouldn't tell anyone his secret name except for you."

She extended the stuffed dog from her lap. "Blake also told me I could have it if I gave it to you for a while if you asked for it."

"We won't keep it long," King said, reaching for it. He thought the urgency inside him should have eased, now that they had figured out the next step along the path that Blake had prepared for them before drowning. But it was the opposite. Each step might be one step closer to King learning something he didn't want to learn about his dad. Besides, holding the stuffed dog didn't exactly give him any idea of what the remote control was for. Maybe something hidden inside the stuffing?

King turned it over, looking for a seam or stitching that might show that Blake had hidden something inside the stuffed dog. He shouldn't have done it in front of Samantha, but the urgency seemed to be at a boil.

Maybe the remote control would make the dog move. Or make something inside the dog beep to let him know it was there.

King pulled the remote control from his pocket, pointed, and clicked.

"Where's the nearest fire hydrant?" It was Blake's voice coming from the tiny speaker that hung from the dog's collar.

"Cool," Samantha said. "How'd you do that?"

CHAPTER 18

"I've never been in an airplane," King told Johnson. "And I've never admitted that to anyone. Except you. Now."

"No biggie," Johnson said. "I won't tell anyone."

They were on the front porch at King's house. Steady rain dripping on the overhang above. But feeling no chill. The evening was warm.

"That's not my point," King said. "It's not a big deal that I haven't been on an airplane. Lots of kids haven't been on airplanes. It's nothing to be ashamed of."

"Yet you've kept this a dark secret."

"Not dark. Just a secret. Because of how bad I want to be in an airplane. I've been on this island my entire life. Trips sometimes to Seattle, but that's it. Like my parents cocooned me here. I'm busting to break out."

"Going to get all sentimental here, like you want wings?" Johnson asked. "Become a beautiful butterfly?"

"I think this is a good example of why guys rarely share feelings," King said.

"My point too. See how I managed to end the conversation? Now we don't have to share feelings."

"So let me tell you why I was thinking about airplanes," King told him. He was talking a lot and knew why. They were waiting for the iPhone to ping. The one on the table between them. Blake's iPhone. King didn't like the silence.

"Not because you feel like singing a ballad about finding your true self someday?"

"*Sky Mall* magazine. You heard of it? It's on airplanes. People can shop while they're flying."

"When I was little," Johnson said in a dreamy voice, "I wanted to be a ballerina…"

"You made your point already with the butterfly thing."

"…until I found out you had to be a girl to be a ballerina."

King snorted. "Go ahead and tell people I haven't been on an airplane. It will be worth the trade. Because I'm going to love telling them about ballerinas."

"Dreams are fragile," Johnson answered.

King was impressed that he couldn't tell if Johnson was serious or not.

"So I'm thinking," King said. "Blake got his ideas from a *Sky Mall* magazine."

This snapped Johnson into full attention. He glanced at the iPhone and then back to King.

"So when I was googling invisible ink and a special flashlight, it took me to the *Sky Mall* website. Guess what. That's where I had seen Measles before. *Sky Mall* sells stuffed dogs with a voice recorder and remote. You can record anything you want."

"Like 'Where's the nearest fire hydrant?' and 'Don't eat yellow snow'?"

Blake had recorded those lines for Measles.

"So maybe when Blake was flying here from Nebraska," Johnson said, "or any other time, he sees this stuff in a *Sky Mall* magazine and thinks it's a great way to send messages from the dead? Like he was planning to be dead even before he got here?"

"I bet if we could find out when he was on an airplane last, that might mean something. I mean, he didn't stay on the island the whole time. He was gone with his parents once in a while. So maybe he discovered something that *might* be happening on the island before the flight, and while he was thinking about how to send us messages, he read the magazine."

"I've seen the magazines," Johnson said, "And don't freak out that I've been on an airplane and you haven't."

King resisted the temptation to make a smart remark about ballerinas.

"You can browse the magazine as you fly," Johnson continued. "You can place an order, but the stuff needs to be shipped to you."

King shrugged. "He gets stuff sent to him here. No big deal."

"Yet he gives us $2000 to smuggle an iPhone to him?"

"But once he had the iPhone, he could buy stuff through eBay or *Sky Mall*."

King gave another glance at the iPhone. Did he really want it to ping with a message? Because then he'd have to go one step further in betraying his father.

"Send blank email to my name backward at dmsgames.com," Blake's voice had spoken through the stuffed dog's collar. "Where's the nearest fire hydrant? Don't eat yellow snow. Where's the nearest fire hydrant? Don't eat yellow snow. Send blank email to my name backward at dms games.com. Throw a ball and I'll chase it. Wait for a reply. Name backward and get it right the first time. Where's the nearest fire hydrant?"

King and Johnson had argued. Had Blake meant drawkcabe manym@dmsgames.com? Or had he meant ttawekalb@dmsgames.com? Or selsaem@dmsgames.com?

Johnson had suggested sending all three emails. But King had reminded him that Blake's voice from Measles had also told them to get it right the first time. In the end, they'd agreed that Blake must have meant for them to use Measles' name as one last piece of protection. Sam had promised not to tell anyone but King the name. Only he would know what name to put in backward.

So they had sent the blank email, and now they were following the next instruction—"Wait for a reply."

That had led to wondering why Blake was putting them through all these steps before giving them any more information about his accusations about King's dad, which had led to another exhausting half hour with Johnson because all conversations with him eventually got exhausting. Johnson was unique, there was no doubt. After all, King was still trying to tell whether Johnson had been serious about a ballerina dream.

Johnson had said that if Blake really was trying to give them information, he could have just put it in the iPhone right away so they would find it right after finding the password with the flashlight and invisible ink. Johnson thought this was just Blake's way of messing with them.

King wanted to believe Johnson. Really wanted to believe him. King had already lost his mother to a coma. If Mack was doing something criminal, it was like he'd lost Mack too—to something that arguably was worse than a coma. At least with Ella, King would always have great memories and never stop adoring her. If Mack truly wasn't the person he appeared to be, King would always have tainted memories about him.

King had argued that Blake was just setting up a few provisions to make sure that only he and Johnson got the real thing that Blake was waiting to give them. That he'd made sure that nobody but King or Johnson would know they had to use Blake's iPhone to send a blank message to selsaem@dmsgames.com.

And apparently, they would learn more only *if* they'd used the correct name backward and *if* the email triggered a return email. And apparently, there was no guarantee of when a return email would show up.

King couldn't get something else out of his mind. "Were you dreaming about a pink outfit too?"

"Huh?" Johnson said.

"Ballerina."

"Oh. Yeah. Ballerina. It wasn't that I wanted to dance like a ballerina. I wanted to look like one. That was before I learned that boys were supposed to like cowboy outfits. Society can be so cruel to those of us who dream different dreams, you know."

King had to admire Johnson. King still couldn't tell if the guy was serious or trying to mess with him.

Then the iPhone pinged.

King nearly dropped it as he fumbled to open up the new email.

The email didn't have a message. Instead, just one line, underlined, blue.

http://m.youtube.com/#/watch?v=w8IfHXACIUo&desktop_
uri=%2Fwatch%3Fv%3Dw8IfHXACIUo

There was only one thing to do. Touch the link.
No surprise. It opened to a YouTube video.

CHAPTER 19

The iPhone didn't have a wi-fi connection, so it loaded on the 4G network. Not LTE. As the video loaded, the spinning circle at the top of the screen seemed to hang forever.

"Just to be clear," King said to Johnson, "you're not expecting your parents home for a while, right?"

"Yeah, yeah," Johnson said, eyes on the screen. "Not for a while."

Then, finally, the YouTube video had loaded.

King had been expecting it, but it was still a shock of sorts to see Blake Watt appear on the iPhone screen. Blake was wearing a white T-shirt. His light blond hair was tousled like always. He was wearing his round thin-framed glasses. Hard to believe Blake was gone.

But in a way, he was still alive in assembled data bits. This was, King thought, the new immortality for humans. Scattered across cyberspace, waiting for instant resurrection by those who were still flesh and blood.

"King. Johnson." Blake was holding the phone at arm's length as he spoke into it. "Hope you're doing better than I am. Weird to be talking to you knowing that you're only going to be seeing this if I'm...not around."

With no warning, the screen went black. It took King a second to realize that Blake had pulled the phone in to his body and hidden it.

Then Blake was back.

"Sorry, guys, I thought I heard something."

Blake took an obvious breath. The video was shaking a little as if his hand wasn't steady.

"You know, I rehearsed this so I wouldn't ramble," Blake said. "But still, it seems like there's so much to say and I hardly know where to begin."

King didn't realize he was leaning in to watch the iPhone until Johnson tapped his shoulder and moved him back so they could both see the screen.

"First, I guess, apologies for what it took to get you guys to this video. It's a private video on a secret YouTube account I set up so nobody will find it by accident. I had to run you through all those hoops to make sure that only you two see this. If someone found the phone taped to a tree by accident, or maybe if you guys had given the phone to the warden when you found it, there's no way anyone else but you would get here.

"Second, I guess, is why. You'll find out soon. But even then, you might not believe it. So let me tell you how I got to the island. Then maybe things will make better sense. I stole a bunch of money."

Blake paused. Grinned. "That got your attention, didn't it. Actually, I didn't steal it for me. I'm a white hat—someone who hacks into systems to test them and help out the people who own them. Black hats are malicious. They put in bad software, steal passwords, stuff like that. Anyway, my mom was the president of her bank. I found a way into the bank's system. I moved some money to prove it could be done, and then I moved it back again. I sent the bank an email to let their IT guys know about it so they could fix it."

On the screen, Blake shook his head. "Some moron there leaked it to the press. All they needed to do was fix the problem, but no, suddenly everybody's screaming about it, and now my mom is under heat even though I was doing it to make sure it got fixed before the bank got in trouble. It was stressing her out so bad because nobody could find out who broke into the system or how.

"She was so freaked out, I told her I'd done it, expecting that she would at least keep that secret. But no, she went all ethical about it, and just like that, I'm on probation with a court order not to be around any kind of computers. Mom resigned and Dad quit his university job so they could move me onto an island and work here and make sure I didn't have Internet access."

Blake grinned into the camera. "So thanks, guys, for helping me get back on the Internet with my first iPhone. I had a bunch of PayPal money stashed away, and once I got back online with the iPhone, I was able to order a bunch of other stuff. And I could use the 4G to get online in secret. Slow, but it's better than nothing.

"The thing is, I live to be a hacker. It's like asking a bird not to fly, telling me to keep away from coding software and jumping into systems and hanging out in forums with other white hats."

Blake lost his smile. "I just didn't expect that breaking into the prison software would show me what I learned there. And now you need to keep helping me with this. But there's no way you're going to believe what I found if I just tell you. I've got my computer set up so that once you get to it, you can go through the steps I did, and then you'll believe."

The smile returned. But it was grim.

"Thing is," Blake said, "you're going to have to go into the abandoned prison. Nighttime will be best. Next video link will show you how to get to my stash."

The video went black again. Because it had ended. And a new video began to load. With instructions on what to do next.

It was like the shock of falling into the deadly cold water of Puget Sound that had kept prisoners from escaping for over a century. The water that had drowned Blake. With a shock like that, for a split second, you can't react. And then, all you can do is sputter and gasp.

Johnson broke the silence first. "No way, man. Not. Going. Into. Abandoned. Prison. Ever."

King squared his shoulders. He was thinking about whatever crime Mack had committed that was the reason for all that Blake had done to set this up. No way did he want Johnson to learn what it was.

"Good," King answered. "Because I want to go alone."

CHAPTER 20

McNeil Island Corrections Center opened in 1875 as a territorial facility. Washington had not yet become a state. Later, the Federal Bureau of Prisons had taken over, and finally, the state of Washington began to lease it from the federal government more than a century later. In 1984, the island was deeded to the state. That was the beginning of the end of the largest parts of the facility. Budget cuts led to the closing of the main buildings, a cluster of concrete structures on the southeast corner of the island, near the ferry dock.

This was King's destination.

It hadn't been difficult to leave the house unnoticed by Mack, who, as usual, had hidden himself in the wood shop almost immediately after returning home at the end of his day shift.

King's biggest problem had been containing his impatience. He'd needed to wait until dark, so he hadn't slipped away until 9:30.

He was okay with solitude in the night air, even passing the cemetery. It was empty. Before the island had become a prison, pioneers had lived and farmed here. When the residents were forced to leave in 1936, all the remains in the cemetery had been exhumed and reburied on the mainland.

Not that King believed in ghosts in the first place. At this point, he figured he had enough trouble with everything else in his life that was haunting him. His mother hovered between death and life, and he wasn't even allowed to see her. His father was keeping secrets and living what looked like a Dr. Jeckyll and Mr. Hyde kind of life—posing as a wonderful father who believed in honor and courage and yet was somehow involved in the drowning of one of King's friends.

Nope. The nighttime and the ghosts were not what worried King. Not even the abandoned prison.

It was the threat of what might be hidden inside and what it might tell him about his father.

※

King came in from the west because the east side of the complex held the occupied buildings, called the McNeil Island Special Commitment Center. In other words, a holding tank for deranged loonies. It was where his father worked. King had often looked at the island with Google maps. The buildings were giant triangles. Five of them in a row connected by an external corridor and surrounded by the electric barbed-wire fence.

At the northwest corner of the complex, near the helicopter landing pad, the remainder of the buildings had been shut down and abandoned. This was his destination.

King was armed with a small flashlight and a small canister of pepper spray that he'd stolen from his father's room and hidden against his ankle in his sock.

He was also armed with a door number. In the video, Blake had promised that entrance 15A had a lock that only looked secure. All it would take, Blake had promised, was a simple tug on the lock, and it would pop open.

King moved slowly among the buildings, stopping frequently to listen for footsteps. Prison guards were not likely to be here, but no sense taking risks. At least, unnecessary risks. What he was doing was definitely risky, but King didn't feel as if he had much choice.

He reached the first building in the abandoned cluster. The exterior was rough concrete, more than a century old. The steel doors had peeling gray paint and barely visible numbers that had been sprayed on with a stencil. It didn't take him long to find 15A.

It was bolted shut on the exterior with a huge padlock that

prevented the bolt from sliding open. King gave it a gentle tug, and it popped open as if it had been oiled. He slid the bolt back, and it, too, was smooth and soundless.

This, he thought, did not bode well. So far, every single thing that Blake had promised from beyond the grave had been accurate. That made it all the more likely that whatever was ahead would be equally accurate.

King stood at the door for an entire minute, wrestling with his decision.

It felt no different from when he'd been at the base of the tree in the forbidden zone, knowing that the next step would betray his trust in his father.

He realized he was only kidding himself at this point. Grabbing the lowest branch of that tree had been the point of betrayal. Everything after that was simply a journey down a slippery slope with no chance of stopping himself. King pushed open 15A and shone his flashlight into the empty hallway.

It smelled faintly of urine. Decades ago, the prisoners had been forced to use wood buckets to hold their body wastes. No amount of bleach and paint had been able to remove the stench.

King stepped inside and closed the door. It occurred to him that if someone bolted it shut on the outside, he would be trapped in this building as surely as the long-dead murderers and thieves had once been held captive. But on this slippery slope, the best he could do was to try to control the direction of his fall.

He plunged forward into the darkness.

Five doors down on the right, Blake had said. Push open the cell door and look beneath the bunk bed on the left wall.

And that's where King found it as promised.

A Macbook Air laptop. Beautiful, lightweight, and sleek.

And without a doubt, filled with something nuclear and ready to explode with fallout as poisonous as radiation.

CHAPTER 21

King popped open the laptop computer lid. Difficult not to love a Macbook Air. Gleaming silver keypad. High-resolution screen.

The screen showed a prompt for a password, and King clicked MEASLES onto the keyboard.

The screen was black for a couple seconds, and then Blake Watt's voice broke the silence that had pressed in on King in the small room.

"Don't touch anything on the computer," Blake said. "Wait for it…"

Blake's face appeared in a small square in the upper right-hand quarter of the screen. It was obviously video. Below that square was another one of similar size, with an arrow button for play. The second video was frozen with a view of a hallway and prison cells.

"Here I am," Blake said. "Your tour guide. But really, don't touch anything without my instructions. Wish I could stand in front of you in 3-D, like Princess Leia in Star Wars, but this was the best I could do."

So weird. Taking instructions from someone who was dead and had been waiting for King. Weird, too, thinking that if King hadn't found this, Blake would have patiently waited for centuries to speak to the first person who opened it—like a genie waiting for someone to rub the lamp.

"You'll see that I've got a couple of programs open on the screen," Blake said. "Don't rearrange the windows for the programs, okay? I'll be sending you to different places, and you're going to need to be slow and careful in each program."

King found himself nodding.

"And be patient," Blake said. Well, Blake's video recording. "You're going to be using the iPhone's hotspot for the Internet connection. I've got it running through a proxy server so no one can get this physical location. It means you'll be safe the entire time you're on the computer. But it's not going to have the Internet speed that I'd like.

"So first, go to Settings on my iPhone. Turn on personal hotspot. It won't take long for this computer to detect the wireless and join automatically. While that's happening, click pause on this video and click play on the video below on the computer screen. It's a piece of surveillance video I found when I hacked into the prison's servers. I think it will speak for itself."

Blake hesitated. "And King, I'm sorry you have to see this. But I didn't have much choice. And I knew you'd need to see it yourself to believe it."

How many hours, King wondered, had Blake spent setting all of this up? And then there was the bigger question. Why? What had Blake known that made him think sending messages from the dead would be needed? What had even led Blake to checking out surveillance video?

King knew there was only one way to find out. By listening to Blake.

He put Blake on pause. Blake's face froze in a distorted position.

King clicked play on the other video.

Because Blake had said it was from the prison, it was an easy guess that it was one of the corridors that led to prison cells.

For a few seconds, there was no movement except for the digital numbers that showed the time of the recording.

23:12:12.

23:12:13.

23:12:14.

Military time on a 24-hour clock. That meant the video King was watching had been taken at 12 minutes past 11 at night.

Someone stepped into the view of the camera, walking away from the camera so that the person's face was not in view.

It didn't matter to King.

He knew that person's walk. Solid, with a very slight side-to-side action. And he knew that person's silhouette. Also solid. Wide at the shoulders.

He'd known that person's solid walk and solid silhouette all his life. He could remember riding on those solid shoulders as a boy, holding on to that person's ears as if they were the reins of a pony. He could remember that person laughing along with King during those magical moments, during the years when his father laughed often and loud and without hesitation.

Mack.

King felt his hand move toward the keypad to click pause. Whatever was going to happen next, he didn't want to see.

But how could King leave now? How could King snap the computer lid shut and wonder for the rest of his life why Blake wanted him to watch this video?

King let the video run, aware that he was breathing shallow and loud and in short gasps, as if he were in physical pain because of the dread that filled him.

In the video, King's father stopped in the hallway at a cell door. He reached out and punched in a password to the cell door. Then he turned and walked toward the camera, not glancing up. Just walked and left the prison cell behind him.

The video kept running.

One second. Two seconds. Three seconds.

A huge guy with a shaved head stepped out of the cell. The man hesitated in the doorway. Then, in prison coveralls, he turned and walked away from the camera, his shoulders twice as wide as King's father's solid shoulders.

King glanced at the digital numbers again.

23:13:02.

23:13:03.

23:13:04.

Then the giant prisoner was out of sight of the fixed camera position, and the hallway was empty again.

23:13:05.

23:13:06.

23:13:07.

That's where the video ended.

From 23:12:12 to 23:13:07. Less than one minute had passed.

But enough time for King to witness that his father had committed a federal crime by releasing an unsecured prisoner.

CHAPTER 22

King listened to the *thud-thud-thud* of his heartbeat fill his ears as he stared at the computer screen. Both video windows were paused. Blake's distorted face filled one. The empty prison hallway filled the other.

Those two squares were one above the other. A larger square filled the rest of the screen to the left of those two squares.

King expected the *thud-thud-thud* to lessen. It didn't. He realized that his life had just shifted. Again. He'd lost his mother. Physically. But at least he had memories to cherish. He'd truly just lost his father. He'd lost his father in a way that was far worse than losing his mother. His father was still there physically, but King now saw him in an entirely different way and didn't think he'd ever be able to recover the trust he'd just lost.

His palms hurt.

He looked down and realized he'd been clenching his fists so hard that a couple of his fingernails had cut through the skin.

King let out a long breath.

Then, with a coldness in his heart, he began to play the video with Blake again.

"Sorry, man," Blake said. "I wish it wasn't so. But it gets worse. Otherwise the dead man's switch wouldn't have been triggered. And you wouldn't be here, watching a video that I set up just in case it got worse. King, you can't walk away."

"Yes, I can," King said to the screen.

"Because if you do, everything on this computer is going to be released to the world in 24 hours. If you want to save your father, you're going to have to keep going here. Because they are using your father. If you can stop them, the world will see he didn't have any choice. If you walk away, it's going to look like your father was and is responsible."

Blake looked down and then up.

"So first thing you need to do is go to my website and enter a password. I had a code in place. A trigger. Once you hooked up this computer to the Internet, it sent that code to begin a 48-hour countdown, and if you don't put the password into the website, it will leak everything to the media. Radio. Television. Newspaper. So run your mouse over the browser window that's open to my right, which is your left. Click the mouse to bring the program to the front, then hit return. That's all it takes."

King felt like a zombie. He did as instructed.

The browser popped open. It brought him to a website: www .blakesdms.com. The browser window slowly filled, showing a place to log in with username and password.

"The username is your name, in lowercase," Blake said. "L-y-o-n-k-i-n-g. That's also the password. Once you enter it, you've bought yourself and your father 24 hours. Do it, King. You have less than 60 seconds on this browser window before it shuts automatically and starts the countdown."

King's fingers were shaky. But he managed.

"Good," Blake said. "I know you did it because I'm still speaking to you. I've got this laptop set up for all of its software to self-destruct if you don't follow my steps precisely."

King knew he was being manipulated. Blake—or, more accurately, Blake from the past—was pressuring King to make decisions without having any time to think. But what choice did King have?

"Okay," Blake said. "Now it's time to tell you why I'm doing this. Forcing you to help."

Blake leaned forward. His voice rasped a little. "I've been trying to outthink them, like a chess game. What I won't know until it happens is how they might choose to get rid of me. It's got to be an accident of course. Drowning is my bet. That's how I'd play it if I were them. Make it look like I was trying to get off the island. It's no secret that I fight a lot with my parents. Only natural that I'd run away, right?"

Blake kept leaning forward. "The people we're dealing with are very careful. If they suspect me, then they know my computer skills. And they know what I found out. They'd be stupid to just get rid of me without finding out what I've left behind. They'd suspect that I'd put something in place to leak everything. And that's why I don't think they'd just snuff me without first finding out all that I know and what I've done with what I found."

Blake smiled grimly. "The way I'd play it is find a way to get me off the island and then threaten to kill me if anything was released. But if that's the case, I can't trust them not to just get rid of me after they feel safe. If I tell them about the dead man's switch, they'll make me put in the code every 24 hours until they find a way to hack into my site and block everything. No, King, it's got to be someone from the outside who puts together everything I put together and goes to them and tells them to release me if they want all the information. That's going to be you."

Blake leaned back. "Yes, King. I'm guessing there's a small chance I'm still alive. So here's the million-dollar question. Was there a body at my funeral? Because if there wasn't, I promise you, they are holding me somewhere. And the clock is ticking. For you to save me and to save your father. Because half of your deal with them is for my life. And the other half of the deal is that they are going to protect your dad too from all that he's done. So get ready to hack into your dad's computer."

CHAPTER 23

"Close the top browser window," the virtual Blake said. "I don't need to remind you, do I? The clock is ticking. I've got everything programmed and timed. You have 60 seconds to go to the next step, or everything starts melting here."

King blinked a few times. He was on a roller coaster and feeling so overwhelmed that he couldn't process it all. So it was easier to just do as directed.

"First," Blake said, "under Applications, look for the program called Terminal. Open it now."

Back to being a zombie again, King did it.

"Type this."

Blake held up a piece of paper.

```
ssh user@[216.180.38.184]
```

"If you care to know," Blake said with the paper still in view, "I've already tapped into your dad's computer and opened up System Preferences. From there, I enabled Remote Login and established the authenticity of the host. To get your dad's password, I just ran a program that rips about a thousand passwords a second until it finds a hit."

A second piece of paper came up. Blake's voice said, "Here's the password."

```
awsumday0810
```

Blake didn't state the obvious, and it was a good thing, because quick tears flooded King's eyes. King was born on October 8. Awsum-day October 8. His dad's password was a phrase of love for King. And now King was using it against his dad.

King forced himself to type in the password.

And suddenly he was looking at the screen that was so familiar to King whenever he saw his dad at the computer.

"You're on," Blake's voice said. "What's cool is that there is no way he can tell on his end. Even if he was on his computer right now, you can roam around like the computer is yours. I've set up a mirror on this end."

King heard a flush of joy in Blake's voice. The kid was a hacker. This was what he lived for.

"Now, open a finder window," Blake continued. "You'll see all his folders. Double-click on the folder marked Vacations."

King groaned. Why did every step have to remind him of how bad it was to betray his own father? Vacations had felt like wonderful cocoons—times for just him and his dad and his mom in a special world that exactly fit the three of them. Why did every step have to remind him that he couldn't trust any of those great memories if all along his father had been someone other than the person he appeared to be?

"All the way down inside that folder is one called Mount Rushmore. Open it."

King did. He expected to find folders.

Instead, there were electronic bank statements.

"Open the top statement," Blake's voice said.

There it was. At the top. His father's name. The date showing a 30-day period for the previous month. And a figure at the bottom of the statement showing how much money was in the account.

King had to look three times to believe what was in front of him. The amount was for $253,893.42.

CHAPTER 24

Back outside the abandoned prison, King let out a deep breath beneath the moonlight. He had felt claustrophobic inside, and his calf muscles felt strained from tiptoeing through the empty dark corridors.

When he reached the path that would take him home, a tall figure detached itself from the shadows, blocking the path.

King reacted without thinking. Flight, not fight. He spun and dashed back toward the road that led to the old prison building. Openness and speed seemed safer than trying to run through the trees and thick underbrush.

"King!" came a shout from behind him. King knew that voice. "Don't!"

That's when King knew who had been waiting to ambush him on the path.

His dad. Mack King.

King glanced back and saw that his dad wasn't chasing him.

So King stopped. Forty yards separated them. At that distance, King had a good head start if Mack made a move toward him.

"We need to talk," Mack said.

"You mean you need to lie to me?" King said.

"You were in the abandoned prison," Mack answered. "Why?"

King was slowly moving away from his dad. He didn't know whether he had enough distance to get away if his dad made a move for him. But really, where was King going to go? He was on an island.

"Something crazy and insane bad is happening at night. Trust no one. They will hunt you too."

Sigmund Brouwer

"No," King answered. "Tell me why you followed me."

"It's night," Mack said. He took a step toward King, out of some shadows, and his face became visible in the moonlight. "You snuck out of the house. Of course I would follow you."

"Stay where you are," King said. "Or we stop talking."

King backed away two more steps.

"What has gotten into you?" Mack said. He took another step. "I'm asking why you snuck out and why you went into the old prison. Whatever is happening, I want to help you."

"We are not going to have this conversation," King said. His brain was working frantically. Where on the island was safe? He might be able to get to the road and run fast enough to find a place to hide. But then what?

The decision was taken away from King by a sudden beam of light from behind him that threw a long shadow down the path toward his father.

At the same time, another sharp circle of painfully bright light threw Mack into a silhouette, casting a shadow down the path toward King.

"Both of you," a loud voice commanded. "Hands up and then freeze. Immediately. Or shots will be fired."

King saw his father raise his hands. His father's shadow looked like the outline of an elongated alien. King slowly did the same and formed a similar elongated alien back down the path toward his father.

The shadows at the ends of their arms touched as if their hands had been reaching each for the other.

When King saw that, he felt a moment of revulsion to be unified, even by a trick of light and shadow, with the man who had betrayed all that he pretended to be.

King dropped his hands. He didn't care if he was shot for it. He wasn't going to let that shadow mock him and his bitterness toward his father.

CHAPTER 25

"This is a serious breach," Murdoch told Mack. "There will be some repercussions."

Murdoch was at the steering wheel. He'd just turned off the engine. Three of them sat in Murdoch's open Jeep TJ. They were parked outside King's house. No lights were on inside the hulking black object that no longer represented home to King.

"It was a lark," Mack said. "Kids do stupid things. Ask King. He'll tell you it was just a prank."

"It's not that simple," Murdoch said. "Once you knew he was out after curfew, your responsibility was to call security, not follow him and break curfew yourself."

"Tell him, son." Mack was in the front passenger seat. He turned sideways to look back at King. "You were goofing around, breaking into the old prison."

"Goofing around?" Murdoch said. He held up the closed Macbook Air. "I think it's a little more than that. We'll need to know why King had this with him."

When the prison guards had frisked both of them, they'd discovered the Macbook Air that King had tucked into his belt at his back, hiding it beneath his shirt as he left the old prison building.

Murdoch also twisted sideways to look in the backseat. "We'll need a little help from you on this, King. It's got a password. How do we access the computer?"

King said nothing from the backseat of the Jeep. Even now, much as he felt bitterness against his father, King couldn't quite take that last step to let the warden know what King had discovered.

"I wish I could tell you," King said. "I tried a few passwords. And then something came up on the screen that said if the next attempt was wrong, a computer program would kick in and erase everything on the computer."

There. That had just purchased some time. The warden was going to be very, very careful with that computer and would probably need to bring in some experts to see what to do next.

"Then tell me," Murdoch said. "Whose computer?"

King didn't answer.

"How did you know it was there?" Murdoch asked.

King didn't answer.

"The kid was there on a lark," Mack said. "Just discovered it by accident."

Silence still seemed like the best option, so King maintained it.

"Here's what we're going to do," Murdoch said as if he were tired and sad about everything. "Mack, I'm going to leave you here. I'm going to take King up to the SCC, and he and I are going to have a long discussion. I'll bring him back in a few hours, and we'll go from there."

SCC. Special Commitment Center. The five high-security buildings inside the forbidden zone.

"Not a chance," Mack said. "You will not separate me from my son."

"You don't have much choice."

Mack spoke to King. "You need to trust me on this. We have to stay together."

Trust, King thought. *What a joke.*

"Enough, Mack," Murdoch said. "Out of the Jeep."

"No," Mack answered. He spoke again to King. "I don't know what's happening, but you need to choose me, not Murdoch."

King thought of what it would be like. Getting out of the Jeep with Mack. Watching the Jeep drive away. Spending the night alone. In the dark house. With a man who let violent prisoners out of their cells late at night and who had a secret bank account with more than a quarter of a million dollars.

It nearly killed King to say it, but it came out anyway.

"No," King said to Mack. "I want to go with Murdoch."

Mack made a slight anguished cry.

"Out," Murdoch told Mack. "I'll see you when I get back with King."

"The same way Blake returned? You're going to have to kill me before you take away my son." Mack threw a punch without warning.

Murdoch's head snapped against the glass of the driver's window. It was a solid thud. Murdoch was motionless.

"Run," Mack hissed at King. "You've got to get away. You can't end up like your mother. I'll stay and deal with him."

Mack fumbled with his seat belt to pop it loose.

That's when King heard a sizzling zap. Mack began to convulse. It took King a moment to realize what was happening.

The official name for the weapon is Electronic Immobilization Device. EID. It's shaped like a pistol. It isn't a Tazer stun gun. Tazers fire a dart and send voltage down the wire connected to the dart.

EIDs are different. They need to be pressed and held against the target to deliver current. They shoot voltage about 450 times the strength of a household current. The longer they are held in place, the longer they incapacitate the target.

Which right now was Mack.

Murdoch hadn't been knocked out by the punch. He'd pulled a stealth move, pretending to be out and then slipping out the EID to press it against Mack and pull the trigger.

"Stop!" King screamed. Mack had already taken at least ten seconds of voltage. "Stop!"

He reached through the gap between the seats to claw at Murdoch's arm. Murdoch pulled back.

Mack sagged against the passenger door. His arms made jerking motions, and his head flopped uselessly.

"King," Murdoch said. "I'm so sorry. But what choice did I have?"

Murdoch started the engine. "And I'm sorry about this too. But we're going to have to put your father in an SCC cell until we bring in some authorities from off the island. What he just did was far more than breach curfew. Your father just moved into felony territory."

"Wait," King said. "I know the password to the computer. And there's something on it you need to see. It's from Blake."

"Blake Watt?" Murdoch shut the engine off.

"Something's happening on the island," King said. He quietly unfastened his seat belt, making sure to talk loudly so Murdoch wouldn't hear the slight snap of release. "Something bad. Blake was putting together information on it. Everything is on the laptop."

"And you've got the password."

"Yeah," King said. He was waiting for Murdoch to open the lid. The light from the screen would be a distraction.

Murdoch lifted the laptop. He began to open the lid.

That's when King leaned down a little and reached for his sock. No way would he have even thought about this in an enclosed space. Because then it would be just as bad for him as Murdoch.

But the Jeep was open to the night sky.

"What's the password?" Murdoch demanded. His eyes were on the screen.

King straightened.

"Pepper spray," King said.

"Pepper spray?" Murdoch turned slightly to King.

King held his breath, closed his eyes, and punched the spray button on the little canister he'd just taken from his sock.

He was rewarded by a scream of agony from Murdoch.

Still holding his breath and eyes still closed, King reached up for the Jeep roll bar and pulled himself into a standing position. Using the roll bar as a guide, he stepped onto the fender and then jumped away from the Jeep.

Then, finally, away from any droplets of the spray, he looked back at the Jeep. Murdoch was clawing uselessly at the sky above him.

King pulled open the driver's door and yanked Murdoch by the collar, and Murdoch sprawled onto the ground and began to vomit.

King held his breath again and felt around inside the Jeep. Bingo. The EID.

The electric pistol felt great in his hand. He leaned down and zapped Murdoch, who gurgled in renewed agony and more convulsions. He gave Murdoch a full 20 seconds, matching what Murdoch had given Mack.

Then King went back to the Jeep to help his father.

CHAPTER 26

"I love you, son."

Not the first words King expected from Mack when King stepped back into the house holding a roll of duct tape he'd just put to good use.

Mack was standing at the kitchen table, hands solid on the tabletop, arms splayed. He was panting as he tried to regain his energy.

"I love you, son."

King was panting himself as he stared at his father. King had expected questions. Like "Where did you go?"

Answer: I drove the Jeep about a quarter mile away, off the road and into some bushes where it might be hard to find, and then ran back to the house.

Or "Where is Murdoch?"

Answer: Duct taped into a tube. Rolled under some bushes at the side of the house. Well hidden.

Or "What are we going to do now?"

Answer: I don't know. Run, I guess. Find a way to keep you out of jail (even though you deserve it) because watching Murdoch zap you with the EID filled me with a rage beyond anything I could comprehend, and I realized that yes, I love you too, but I don't want to say it. Or say that I love you so much that even though you're doing something criminal on the island, I will protect and hide you.

Mack croaked out his next words. "And I'm saying I love you because if we don't get off this island alive, it's something you need to know, and I should have said it a lot earlier."

"Yeah," King said. "Well, I hate talking about it too. And some things you don't need to say because you prove it every day. Okay? Now, how are we going to fix things?"

Then Mack asked the expected question. "Where did you go?"

After zapping Murdoch with the EID, King had gone to the passenger side of the Jeep and lifted Mack out and half dragged him into the house and onto a couch. Mack's body had been trembling with after-effects of the shock.

"Hid Murdoch first. He's rolled up in duct tape under a bush. I waited until he finished all his puking and then taped up his mouth too. Didn't want him to puke into the duct tape and drown. Put tape over his eyes too. Wish I could be there when they pull the tape away and rip out his eyebrows. I wanted to kill him for hurting you."

Mack managed a weak snort. He tried to stand straight. Couldn't. He leaned on the table again. "I might need a few more minutes. The Jeep. You moved it."

Not a question. A statement. Like Mack trusted him to be smart.

"They're going to come looking for us," King said. "They're expecting you and Murdoch out at the SCC anytime. This is going to be the first place they check, right?"

Neither of them wasted time with the other questions yet. Both of them had obviously stepped over a line, and there was no going back. Escape first. Then the luxury of second-guessing whatever they had done.

"My closet," Mack said. "Black sweat pants, shirts, and shoes. Get a set for you and for me. Look on the top shelf. Black shoe polish. Grab a facecloth. We're going to need it for our faces."

Again, no time for questions, including why Mack would have that stuff.

When King got back, Mack was standing without the table for help, taking deep breaths.

King threw sweat pants, a jersey, and the can of shoe polish on the table.

"Not dressing you," King said.

"Not going to let you," Mack said.

This felt good to King, his new role as an equal to his father. King stripped down to his underwear, dropping his clothes on the floor.

King was faster getting dressed than Mack. Of course, he hadn't sustained 20 seconds of electric voltage to short-circuit his neurons.

"Run next door," Mack said. "Get that stupid dog. Bring it back."

King gave his dad a puzzled look.

"No time to explain. We've got maybe five minutes before they swarm this place."

King ran from the house and slipped into the yard next door, where Patches pulled against the long rope that tethered him to a post in a circle of worn-out grass. Patches gave a little yelp in greeting.

King unsnapped the dog's collar from the rope and dragged Patches back to the house.

Mack had scooped up King's clothes from the floor, put them into a plastic bag, and duct taped the bag into a compressed tube.

"Hold the dog still."

Patches wagged his tail in total noncomprehension as Mack put the plastic bag on the dog's back and began wrapping duct tape around the dog's body to hold it there like a saddle.

"Guessing they tracked you to the old prison by something in your clothes. Probably your jacket. Device would be too small to find easily. If it's in there, they can start looking for you in some strange places."

Mack went to the door and held it open.

"Hey, stupid dog," Mack said. "Freedom."

Patches was smart enough to know what an open door and no leash meant. With a happy yelp, Patches bolted with a scratching of claws on the floor and was gone without looking back.

Mack grabbed the shoe polish.

"Come here," he said to King.

It had been a while since King had been physically this near to his father. They were almost eye to eye as Mack spread shoe polish on King's face and neck. Mack's fingers were strong, pushing hard on King's skin.

"Now me," Mack said, handing the can to King.

Mack maintained eye contact.

"Getting a feeling that you don't like me much right now," Mack said.

"Brilliant," King answered.

"Let's make sure we get a chance to sort it out later," Mack said. "But for now, I think it's best we get moving. That stupid dog isn't going to buy us much time. They're good at tracking things at night."

"Don't we need to take anything?"

"Nope," Mack answered. "Trust me."

CHAPTER 27

They were a hundred yards from the house, jogging inland, when King spoke.

"What's the matter with the shoreline back there?" King asked.

"You say that like you know there's danger."

"You've given this some thought," King answered. "Black sweats, my size, in your closet. Black sneakers, my size. Like you've been ready for us to run."

They were on a gentle rise, headed toward the tree line that started closer to the center of the island.

Mack didn't answer, just kept a good rhythm to their jogging.

"Easy escape," King said, "would be to have a boat hidden as close as possible to our house. Three minutes of jogging gets us to the shoreline, and we're on the water."

This seemed utterly surreal. The two of them on the run. Because King had assaulted the warden with pepper spray and then gone a step further and duct taped him and squirreled him into a bush.

But then it seemed surreal to King that the man he was escaping with had hidden more than a quarter of a million dollars. Money he had earned for reasons that King couldn't even guess. All because a kid who drowned had been sending King on a chase, directed in cyberspace.

No sense thinking about it all, King told himself. Roll with the flow. Or more accurately, jog with the flow.

"I know stuff," Mack finally said. He stopped, barely breathing hard.

"And they know I know stuff. I couldn't tell you. They were using you as leverage. They promised something would happen to you if I let you off the island. It's why you couldn't visit Ella. And that was killing me as much as it was killing you."

Mack put up a hand and cocked his head, listening. He seemed satisfied at what he heard. Or didn't hear.

"And they also threatened Ella's coma would end with her death."

"What!"

"It's like they've got her in a prison," Mack said. "She's helpless and can't move. So I had to pretend everything was normal. I couldn't tell you. Didn't want to tell you. It wasn't that I didn't trust you. I just wanted to protect you."

He waved his hands. "Obviously, things have changed. So yes, I've had an escape plan in mind. Even Murdoch had to admit that if I didn't visit Ella at the hospital once or twice it would look bad. I bought some stuff for escape each trip, and I've done some planning. You would be right about the shoreline. They've got thermal sensors everywhere. Keeping a boat hidden wasn't going to do it. They'd know down to the second when we got into the boat. A minute later, a chopper would be there. We'd be sitting ducks."

Mack began jogging again. "They've got the entire shoreline rigged with sensors. Hidden cameras too. They know if someone gets on the island. Or gets off. The whole island is a prison.

King kept pace. "Except for the northwest corner, right? At the cliffs. That's where we're headed. No point putting sensors there."

There was a stretch of about a half mile where the island rose vertically from the strait. At the top of the rocky cliff, it was a 100-foot drop to jagged rocks in shallow water. Seals loved to congregate beyond the rocks.

"You're wrong," Mack said. "They've got sensors there too in case someone found a way down the cliffs. But yeah, that's where we're headed."

"That's going to take us through the forbidden zone. No way to make it past the thermal sensors."

"Not much choice," Mack said. "At least it will put us in the trees.

Choppers won't get us when we're in that cover. If we move fast, we can get through the zone and to the cliffs before they can send anyone in after us."

"Then what?" King asked.

"One thing at a time," Mack answered.

They were almost at the edge of the trees.

"Mack," King said. "How are we going to protect Mom?"

Mack kept jogging.

King thought Mack hadn't heard. "Mack, what about Mom? You said they were using her as leverage. She's like a prisoner to them. Now they know you're on the run with me. What's the plan to make sure she's safe?"

More jogging.

"Mack—"

His dad stopped again. He put his hands on King's shoulders. "It's what I would have wanted her to do if things were reversed. We both love you more than you can ever know."

"Mack?"

"Don't ask, okay?" Mack started jogging again. Faster. Harder. As if he were trying to outrun a demon.

Then King figured it out. Mack had been forced to choose. Save his wife or save his son.

CHAPTER 28

"Chopper," King said.

They were maybe a hundred yards from the first plateau on the nearest hill, now both breathing hard.

Still, above his panting, King caught the *throb-throb* of the chopper engine—felt it at first more than heard it. King glanced back. Seconds later, just above the house they'd left behind, beams of light cut downward from the night.

And moments after that, headlights from a dozen vehicles broke from the road a hundred yards away and headed toward the house.

This was it. King was on the run. A criminal now. Like his father.

He felt Mack's hand on his shoulder. King hadn't realized he'd slowed down to watch what was happening behind him.

"Faster," Mack said. "They'll come in with onboard thermal sensors next, and the tree cover here isn't deep enough."

A person can't outrun thermal sensors, King thought. They were done.

But he followed Mack.

At the edge of the trees, Mack pulled out a small flashlight. He'd taped most of the lens so that only a pinprick of light showed.

"Nearly there," Mack said.

Again, it struck King how prepared Mack had been, making sure the flashlight gave as little exposure as possible.

Even so, he was startled and amazed about 20 yards later when Mack stopped abruptly, kicked aside pine needles and dirt, and exposed a circular wooden lid with a handle.

Mack grunted as he pulled the lid aside. When he pointed the narrow beam of light downward, King saw that the interior was narrow at the top and wider below. A small ladder was propped against the edge, which had been reinforced with plywood to keep the soil from collapsing.

"Down," Mack said.

King didn't hesitate. He grabbed the top of the ladder and reached the bottom almost immediately. Just as quickly, Mack's shoes were at the bottom rungs. But Mack didn't jump off the ladder. He slid the cover across the top.

Their heavy breath filled the small cavern.

"We'll be good here for a bit," Mack said. "They'll use the chopper to sweep with searchlights because they'll think they're tracking you, not Patches. It'll take them, what, five minutes to find that stupid dog?"

"Sure," King said. His mind was more on this cavern than Mack's conversation. Especially because Mack had been using the flashlight to spot various items that were stacked against the side. A couple of EIDs. Two rifles. Rope. Flares.

"After they find Patches and realize what we did to distract them, they'll go to thermal sensors from the chopper. Any luck and tonight would have had drizzle. Water droplets deflect the infrared and make it hard to spot anything more than a quarter mile away. But it's a clear night, so the range goes up to about two miles. But that can work for us too. They'll make a couple of passes with sensors, and once they don't find our thermals, they'll move on. We'll use that window of time to get to the wildlife refuge. Those trees are old growth. Thick canopies. Next to impossible to get any thermals from the choppers."

"That's the forbidden zone," King said. "They've got sensors everywhere at ground level."

"Got it covered," Mack said. His flashlight beam picked up a cell phone near the stack of equipment. Mack grabbed it and turned it on. "Once I send a text, we've got one hour with the system down. Someone owes me a huge favor, and I'm calling it in. And that's all we need. One hour."

"Plus this stuff that will put down anyone who chases us," King said, motioning at the electric pistols and the rifles.

"That's the part I wish I didn't have to explain," Mack answered.

He sat and leaned back against the dirt wall. King did the same.

"It started about a year ago," Mack said. "When they closed down the old prison and brought in a bunch of new guards for the SCC. Remember when I was permanently put on day shift? That's because it always happens at night."

CHAPTER 29

"I'd come in some mornings," Mack continued, "and something would be wrong with one of the prisoners in solitary. He'd have bruises or cuts. I'd ask Murdoch about it, and he'd tell me that the prisoner had acted up the night before and that one of the night guards had to settle him down."

Mack paused. "Thing is, when I'd ask the prisoner what had happened, he couldn't tell me. Not *wouldn't* tell me, but *couldn't*. Like his mind was a blank."

King could feel sweat trickling down his chest. His body was cooling down after the jog.

"Then one morning, I noticed spruce needles in one of the cells. Spruce. And what looked like spruce sap in his hair. Crazy, I told myself, but I decided not to say anything about it. The night crew guards, they were a different breed. Kept to themselves. Almost like they looked down on the day guards. I wasn't going to ask them, and I knew Murdoch didn't like my questions either. So I decided to find out without asking questions."

Mack flashed his beam of light back at the equipment. It settled on what looked like a pair of binoculars.

"Night vision goggles. Best you can buy. I found a good spot outside the forbidden zone, away from the thermal sensors. I settled in one night and watched through the goggles. I was ready for a lot of nights of watching. If—and that was a big if to me—if a prisoner was getting outside at night, I had no way of knowing where he'd leave the building. I got lucky with my first guess. The loading docks."

King imagined Mack tucked away on a hillside, patient for hours.

"First a chopper comes in. Some guy I've never seen before steps out. Civilian. Pulls out a rifle bag. Has two dogs with him. Murdoch is there to meet him. Ten minutes later, two of the night guards escort out Lassiter—one of the prisoners. You got to understand, Lassiter is a monster. Physical monster. Inhuman monster. Shaved head, neck as thick as an elephant's leg, tattoos across his face...he looks like Spiderman. Things he did to get put here...you wouldn't sleep for a week if I told you. Guards point Lassiter at the trees and let him go. Just like that. Then the warden, the guy with the dogs and the rifle, the guards, all of them, they just stand around. Half hour goes by. The warden shakes the guy's hand, and the guy heads into the trees with his two dogs."

Mack went silent for a bit, as if right back on the hillside, watching. King had a guess but didn't want to say it.

Mack picked up the story again. "I stay. I mean, there's nowhere to go anyhow. I don't dare draw attention to myself. Four hours later, one of the night guards heads out in an ATV. Half hour after that, he gets back. The civilian on the passenger side, broken arm, only one dog with him. Lassiter's body is on the back of the ATV. I think Lassiter's dead."

Mack's voice went cold. "It was a game. Hunt down the prisoner. Next morning, I'm at Lassiter's cell. He's cut up a bit, got some stitches on his right hand. Looks like a dog bit him. But he's groggy. I ask him how it's going, did he get a good night's sleep, and nothing registers in his eyes. It's like he doesn't know anything about what happened the night before."

"They catch you catching them?" King asked. He didn't know whether to believe Mack. The part about hunting down prisoners, yeah, that was probably true. Blake Watt had been leading King up to this through cyberspace. But Mack was talking as if he were an outsider. King had seen the video surveillance footage and seen the money in Mack's bank account.

"I was careful," Mack said in answer to King's question. "They didn't know I knew. I start keeping track. As far as I can tell, one prisoner a week gets outside. Every once in a while, a whole group. Six or seven.

I keep careful notes, and then when I think I've almost got enough to go to the FBI in Seattle, I get caught. I'm expecting Murdoch to do something crazy to protect his secret, but instead, he calls me into his office and calmly explains that if I breathe a word, I'll be in jail for ten years. Next thing I know, Ella's in a coma, and Murdoch tells me you're next if I don't do everything I'm told. That's when I had to start keeping secrets from you."

"And keep me on the island."

"They made it clear it wouldn't be good for your health." Mack's voice broke. "I mean, look what happened to Blake. He found something, didn't he. And passed it on to you."

"The computer in the old prison," King said. "He had stuff on there."

"Yeah, Murdoch was ready to make you disappear." Mack shifted his body. "Where's the computer?"

"Safe," King said, realizing he didn't fully trust Mack.

"We'll need it," Mack said. "Just not now. First thing we need to do is get to the cliffs."

"Then what?" King asked.

Mack explained.

And that's when King realized exactly how much planning Mack had done.

CHAPTER 30

Mack handed King one of the rifles. It weighed less than King expected.

"No bullets," Mack said. "Darts. Let me show you how to use it." Mack took King through the bolt action and showed him how to load the darts.

"No bullets?" King asked. "Darts don't have much range."

"For starts, too much noise," Mack answered. "Noise of a gunshot will bring a full force in on us. Besides, we don't want to kill anyone. We're not hunting, so we don't need a long-range shot. You don't need blood on your hands for the rest of your life. Or a murder-one felony."

Something clicked for King. "The prisoner hunt. This is what they use, isn't it. Dart guns. Otherwise, we'd hear gunshots on the island at night when they turn the prisoner loose. Darts won't kill them either."

It made sense. On this island, 103 of the most dangerous felons in North America. For a big-game hunter who was willing to pay tens of thousands of dollars to hunt a grizzly, how much more of a thrill to hunt a human, the deadliest predator of all.

"Yes, it's what they use," Mack confirmed. His voice was flat. "Some of the hunters ask for a prisoner to be given a weapon. A knife maybe. Or a dart gun. Gives the hunters an even bigger thrill, hunting someone who is hunting them."

King thought of the money hidden in his father's bank account. "They pay a lot, won't they."

"Yeah."

King thought of something else. "You said we're not hunting. That means then we have these weapons for defense."

Mack's silence was enough of a confirmation.

"Who is going to hunt us?" King asked.

"Guards don't know the terrain as well as the prisoners," Mack replied.

Some of the most dangerous men in America. "So this will be life or death," King said.

"Has been for a lot longer than you've known," Mack answered.

Long, long silence.

"Dying scare you?" King asked.

"Not as much as it makes me sad. Too much in life to hold on to. You, mainly. Your mother and I…" Mack's voice grew quieter. "We had no idea what love really was until you were born. Didn't have any idea of what fear was either. And let me tell you, when you're scared of losing something, there are so many things to worry about. Dryer lint, for one."

"Dryer lint?"

"You were maybe a year old. I'd be up two or three or four times a night, and I'd go into your room just to listen to you breathe when you were sleeping. Sweetest sound I can remember. I was watching you, and it hit me. What if there was a buildup of lint in the dryer and it caught on fire? What are the chances? A billion to one? But I couldn't get it out of my mind. It's three in the morning, and I'm in the laundry room, checking all the vents to make sure they were clear of lint. Ella woke up and asked what I was doing. When I told her, she didn't laugh. She started helping me check the vents."

King smiled in the dark, but at the same time, it made him sad. Ella. Alone. And that thought terrified him now. Murdoch had threatened to do something to Ella. King and Mack had to find a way to stop it. They had to get past the thermal sensors and through the forbidden zone. They had to escape the island, find a way to make Ella safe.

"Kids don't know how much parents love them," Mack continued, obviously unaware of the lurch of fear inside King. "Good thing, or you'd be paralyzed. What am I going to do, stop you at the door on your way to kindergarten and tell you that if anything happened to you and you didn't come back from school, I'd be a broken man for the rest of my life? And believe me, a parent can come up with a thousand things to worry about, from earthquake to fire to a bus driver not paying attention. So then, what? Kneel down and look in your little five-year-old face and put my hands on your shoulders and tell you to be very, very careful because you've got my heart in your hands, and if you don't make it home, I'll be dead inside for the rest of my life, and I'll spend three hours a day sobbing in uncontrollable tears? Not a chance. You'd look at me and offer to sit on the couch and wrap yourself with pillows and never leave home, just so Daddy doesn't have to cry. And if you offered to sit on the couch and be safe, the biggest part of my heart would want to accept the offer. King, parents lay awake at night when their teenagers are at a party. We worry about a phone call from the police or a knock at the door that starts with 'Sir, I'm sorry to tell you…'"

This was more than his dad had spoken in one time to him than King could remember. And here King was, unable to escape another thought. About the money in his father's bank account and the surveillance video that showed Mack releasing a prisoner.

"I can't make you have faith in God," Mack said. "And even if you said it was there, that's still something between you and God. But I want you to know why I believe. It began the moment I held you. Your tiny head was in my palm, and the rest of your body stretched along my forearm with your toes touching the inside of my elbow. I busted out bawling. I couldn't remember the last time I'd cried. I'm holding you and bawling my eyes out and so full of this insane love…I decided that love was bigger than my pitiful little life and that it gave meaning to everything I did.

"To me, it's about starting with a search for how and why life has meaning. There I was, holding you, and I finally understood the phrase I'd heard again and again so often it had become hollow up to that moment: God loves you like a father loves a son. Like a parent loves a child. And I figured if you couldn't ever realize how much I loved you, then that's how it must be for God and how He loves me. I'm not saying you need to be the kind who shakes his fist at anyone who doesn't agree. I'm just saying I hope you'll give a long hard look at whether there's more to this life than what you see in the physical world. Here's my biggest and sometimes my only prayer. That whatever happens in this lifetime, we'll be a family beyond."

"You're scaring me," King said.

"I know. We don't talk like this very much. Okay, never. But you got to admit, a place and time like this leads you toward it."

"It's not that," King said. "It's what I'm reading between the lines. You're worried about the dryer lint again. Except this time, it's not a chance in a billion. We're armed with dart rifles and EIDs, and we've got about five miles of wilderness and deranged killers between us and the cliffs. And we're having this talk because you don't like our chances of making it."

Mack hesitated and then gave a half smile. "Yep. What I'd give to be back in that moment when I thought things were in my control and that cleaning the dryer vents would be enough to protect you. But I learned that control is just an illusion. All we can do is our best."

"Probably a good time for a hug," King said.

"Yeah, but that would be awkward. So let's check our weapons instead. That favor I called in…the sensors won't be down very long."

CHAPTER 31

"Snorkeling gear?" King asked Mack as he looked inside the backpack. "Wet suit?"

Mack had set out a battery-powered lantern, and the light seemed soft in their bunker as King looked through the contents. It was a full-size camping backpack made of nylon fabric—black, of course—with a lightweight aluminum frame.

Mack had taken the backpack from where it leaned against the wall, handed it to King, and invited King to open it and peer inside. A second backpack—from all appearances, identical—was still along the wall. This one belonged to Mack.

"I've got a matching suit in my backpack," Mack said. "The only way to survive the water is to keep from getting too cold. The wet suits will also keep us buoyant. Flippers and mask and snorkel will make it easier for us to swim."

"And stay underwater with just a snorkel showing if a chopper has searchlights? The black wet suit doesn't hurt either."

Mack grunted in agreement. Then he motioned at the backpack. "Front pocket. Put the GPS watch on your left wrist."

King did as instructed. It had a rubber wristband, clear plastic face, and rubber coating around the face. Black, naturally.

Mack reached over to the lantern and shut it off. The bunker went black.

"Learn to read it in the dark," Mack said. "Feel for the three buttons on the side. In home position, top button brings up the compass.

Middle button shows a couple of GPS waypoints that I've set. Bottom button gives a little arrow. Click the middle button."

King's eyes had begun to adjust to the dark. He saw the numbers in glowing green, showing the time. When he clicked the middle button, the numbers transitioned to A, B, C.

"Top button brings up A," Mack said. "Middle button brings up B. Bottom button gives you C. We want to get to A first, so press the top button."

When King did, the green glowing numbers changed again. He understood the top number. It was the GPS waypoint. Below it was a small arrow. And under that another number: 1575.

"Five minutes," Mack said. "That's when we leave this bunker. The chopper will have cleared the area, and we won't have to worry about heat sensors from above. That gives us 20 minutes to go about one and a half kilometers to reach position A while the thermal sensors are down."

"That's what I'm reading?" King asked. "Fifteen hundred seventy-five meters to the destination?"

"Meters," Mack confirmed. "Kilometer and a half is about a mile. I've set the GPS to metric. See that arrow? It points to the target. No way to get lost. Just follow the arrow and check once in a while to see how the gap is closing."

"Sounds easy."

"It is easy. I have my own. In case we get separated, we meet at position B. That's by the cliff, in a gap between sensors."

"Are ropes there so we can climb down?"

"No, I've got flares, duct tape, and a bunch of other stuff in my backpack. We're going to fly. It's like MacGyver."

"Fly? MacGyver?"

King was rewarded by a sigh from Mack.

"MacGyver. A guy in a television series who engineered escape plans."

"And position C?" King asked.

"Mainland. Hiding spot on the shore. When we hit the water, we use the watches to make it across to where I buried a garbage bag with clothes and money. I made sure it's where the current will take us as we swim across. In the water, all we need to do is check the arrows on the GPS occasionally to make sure we're in position as we swim."

King thought of the dark, cold water and shuddered. Not likely that sharks would be cruising. But he'd have to trust what he'd heard about killer whales. That there were no recorded attacks on humans. Of course, if people didn't survive a killer whale attack, they wouldn't be around to report it.

King had a question, but Mack didn't give him a chance to ask.

"Side pocket," Mack said. "Night vision goggles. I don't want to turn the lantern back on and ruin your night vision. The longer we're in here like this, the easier on our eyes when we go back outside. Put the goggles on and find the switch at the left side."

King found the goggles. Hit the switch.

"Cool," King said. The total dark had gone to a greenish glow as it picked up the tiny bit of light shed by the GPS.

"Drop them around your neck for now, okay? If you're not used to them, it makes it tougher to walk, and we should have enough moonlight to get to position A. My goggles are thermal sensors. When our targets are close enough, that's when we'll put on the goggles, and between thermal and visual, we should have the advantage."

"Targets?"

"No way are we going to make it to the edge of the cliff without Murdoch sending hunters after us. These men are experienced hunters and killers. The sane thing to do would be to run as fast and as hard as possible. Last thing he's going to expect is for us to do the hunting first. We take them out before they take us out, and by the time he gets a second set after us, it's too late. We win the race to the cliff."

"Position A," King said. Humans hunting humans. The thought of it sent his already racing heart into overdrive, and he felt a new surge of adrenalin. The most dangerous predator in the world was also the most dangerous prey. "We're setting up an ambush?"

"Yeah," Mack answered. "With about a half hour to get there. You ready?"

"Not much choice," King said. "Not anymore."

CHAPTER 32

"If we get into position before the hunters are released, we'll have a chance."

That had been Mack's promise. Of course, it depended on whether the favor Mack had called in had been delivered and the thermal sensors stayed down the entire hour, giving them a small window of time to make it unnoticed into the forbidden zone. And it depended on how long the western-facing rock wall behind King held the heat it had absorbed during the day.

King stood near the base of a spruce tree beside that wall, well covered by low-hanging branches. His dart rifle rested on a branch, and the barrel stuck out of the dense spruce needles and faced the path. He could reach the trigger almost instantly.

The branches provided a visual screen for an ambush, especially at night, even if the hunters had night vision goggles. Still, King felt open and exposed. He knew his body heat was higher than the heat of the tree. He felt as if he and Mack were easy targets for anyone who was using thermal sensors or receiving instructions from someone at the prison's main computer terminal.

To get around that, King was wrapped in a space blanket. This common camping item, based on NASA technology, was a lightweight plastic sheet with a Mylar coating that made it look like tinfoil. But it was lighter and cheaper, and it was a great reflector of heat.

King was wearing it inside out, to minimize any leakage of body heat that would reach a thermal sensor. He also wore a hood crudely made from the same material. With the night vision goggles on, most of his face was covered.

His best protection, however, was the 12-foot-tall outcropping of rock wall behind him, rock that had absorbed heat during the day and was cooling gradually now.

When they'd reached it, Mack had reassured King by giving King a look at the rock face through his thermal goggles. The rock wall— virtually invisible in the darkness—glowed a dull orange in the thermal goggles. As further reassurance, Mack had stepped up to the rock and wrapped himself in a space blanket, and King had checked it out through the thermals. Mack's heat imprint was lost against the heat imprint of the rock.

Perfect. Well, almost perfect.

The space blanket was crinkly, so it rustled with the slightest movement. Which meant King had to remain perfectly motionless as the space blanket reflected his body heat back at him and drops of sweat trickled between his shoulder blades and collected in the small of his back.

King was terrified, and this alone was enough motivation not to reveal himself with movement. But he was also determined to be Mack's equal. If Mack could hold position in total silence and total patience under another spruce only five yards farther down the path, then King would do it too.

The loudest thing, it seemed to King, was his own heartbeat. Because if Mack was correct, Murdoch had sent out some of the most disturbed men in the entire national prison system. With the sole purpose of hunting Mack and King.

"If we get into position before the hunters are released, we'll have a chance."

It also depended on whether the released prisoners followed the pattern Mack had observed earlier. He'd told King that they usually fanned out in pairs. One pair always took the path that led past this rock outcrop because it was the easiest route into the heart of the forbidden zone.

It was a gamble, but it was really their only option.

With Mack's dart rifle set in position too, all they could do was wait. And hope.

Predator was now prey.

CHAPTER 33

They came in as delicately as mice afraid of attracting a cat.

Two of them, just as Mack had predicted. He'd always observed them hunting in pairs.

What made the delicacy of their approach more terrifying was how big each of the men were. King had been straining to see the slightest movement through his night goggles, and at first, he thought the slight detachment of a shape from a tree down the path was his imagination.

Then he realized it was worse than anything he could imagine in a nightmare.

The shape turned into the vague outline of arms and legs attached to a huge body. Then a second body.

King stopped breathing.

He had specific instructions from Mack. *"Don't shoot. Let them pass."*

King's role was backup. Mack would take them out.

King waited until it felt as if he had to gasp. Mack had thermal goggles. *Surely Mack had seen them, right?* But nothing was happening.

Except the vague terrifying outlines of two humans moved closer and closer. Any second now, they'd reach Mack and—

The crinkle of movement came first. The Mylar betrayed that Mack had made his move.

The slightest shift of time. Then, *thfft, thfft.*

Mack had fired the dart rifle.

So close to that sound that King almost didn't hear came the *slap, slap* of darts striking targets.

Then snorts of laughter from the monsters on the path.

"Dude," one of them said in a weirdly echoing voice. "That all you got?"

In the moonlight, King could see their outlines clearly through his night vision goggles, green ghostly images that looked like Sasquatch. They split apart, forming a triangle of the two of them and the position from where Mack had fired, transforming themselves from mice scared of a cat, to cats themselves, twitching tails and about to pounce.

King couldn't figure it out.

The darts had hit each of them. He'd heard it happen.

But neither had seemed affected.

"Come out, come out, wherever you are," a second voice taunted in the same weirdly echoing voice, as if this were a childhood game of hide-and-seek. "We're going to hurt you bad. Murdoch said we could make this terminal. We love our knives. Just like the others out tonight looking for you."

One of them passed by King so close that King could have prodded the huge man with the tip of the barrel of his dart rifle.

That's when King made his decision without even thinking about it.

Reaching down to the small of his back where he'd tucked his EID pistol, King leapt out in a rush of fury and fear and held the trigger tight, knowing as soon as it made contact, it would paralyze the largest of monster humans.

He was hampered by his night vision goggles, which scraped against the branches as he dove through, moving the goggles away from his eyes. But his hands made contact, and that's what guided his attack.

He jammed the electric pistol into the bulk of the man's body. Instinct, based on his memory of how the jolt had crippled Murdoch, told him he'd succeeded.

Then King's brain told him otherwise, that his instinct was wrong.

The animal—because in essence, that's what was in front of him, one of the biggest mammals on the continent, smaller than only bears—whirled upon King and with a roar, brought a fist into King's chest.

King stumbled backward, as much in disbelief that the electric pistol had failed as in surprise at the counterattack. And with the quickness of any other savage beast, his attacker lunged.

King's paralysis served him well. But by accident.

He'd been too surprised to release the electric pistol, too surprised to unclench his trigger finger.

When the man fell on King, King pushed upward in panic. That's when the man's roar of anger turned into a gurgle of flailing helplessness. Finally, King's gun had made contact.

King rolled with the man and dimly understood why his first effort had failed. His free hand brushed against a nylon fabric, and as he punched, it gave solid resistance. Kevlar?

No time to think more.

Feel for the man's throat.

That's where King must have hit him by accident the first time, and now, with primal rage and fear driving him, King jabbed the electric current back into the man's throat again.

The man's flailing became shortened spasms, and King pulled himself out of his rage and let his brain take over again.

One more attacker. But where?

He flipped to his feet and looked around. With his goggles off, he saw only darkness. Until an impact against the side of his head sent bright lights across his vision.

He tumbled. Tried to jab upward. Not. Good. Enough.

The full weight of the second man was upon him, a crushing sensation as horrible as a landslide. King's arms were pinned, and he had no chance of using the electric pistol to protect himself.

Then hands against his own throat. A squeezing that felt like it was crushing cartilage. Lights that burst inside his retina, then dimmed.

Until…

Out of the darkness, another scream of rage. A massive thump. Another massive thump. Neither thump dislodged the beast that was killing King.

Then the body on top of King flailed, quivered, and spasmed.

The scream of rage became a calm voice.

"King. You okay?"

King could only manage a grunt. His lungs felt as if an elephant were standing on his chest.

Mack grunted too, but his was a grunt of effort. He was pulling at the shoulders of the second man, trying to roll him off King. King twisted and rolled the other way. Finally, air. Sweet clean air.

King gasped a few times and then got to his knees.

"What took you?" King managed to say, leaning over with his hands on his knees.

"Tactical error," Mack said. Mack was panting but managed to speak clearly. "I hit him as hard as I could with my backpack. Had it by the straps and swung it as hard as I could. Twice. Didn't work. I had to jump him and find a spot to jab him with my electric pistol."

By then, Mack was using his flashlight to play it across the two fallen men. It confirmed what King had guessed.

Kevlar vests. Bulletproof. And dart proof.

Each man wore night vision goggles and a helmet with a face shield, which explained why their voices had sounded so weird. A dart wouldn't have brought one down unless it hit him in the few square inches of exposed neck.

"We need to stay close to each body," Mack said. "Remember?"

Their plan had been to make it into the forbidden zone undetected, then bring down a couple of the men hunting them. The heat sensors weren't able to distinguish individual men, let alone individual features.

Now with those men down, all they needed to do was drag the men to the rock face and cover them in thermal blankets. Those two would become invisible, and Mack and King could move freely. Whoever was monitoring the thermal sensors would believe Mack and King were the two men who had left the prison. And to anyone monitoring their movement, their travel to the cliff's edge would look like a natural part of the hunting pattern.

Except now there was one slight problem.

CHAPTER 34

"Mack," King said, "these guys will be unconscious ten minutes at most. Maybe less. Big as they are, they could wake up any second. The EIDs won't keep them out as long as a dart would."

Mack let the flashlight roam, showing again helmets, visors, and the Kevlar.

"We'll have to hit them with darts," Mack said. "But if we shoot them in the throats at this range, it will kill them. Tempting, but not a memory either of us needs."

"Shine the light on one of the legs, okay?"

King had a jackknife in his pocket. He knelt and tried cutting through the fabric of the first man's pants.

No luck. The fabric was a tight nylon that would have resisted darts too. "Suggestion?" King asked.

Mack sighed. "It's going to have to be a couple of butt shots. Unbuckle their pants."

"You didn't just say 'butt shot,' did you?" King wanted to giggle, probably a reaction to the stress he'd just faced.

"Look, that's what doctors do, right? Give you a needle in the—"

"No." King groaned. "Bottom of their feet. That's better than a butt shot, right?"

King didn't wait from an answer from Mack. He untied the first man's left boot and pulled it loose.

Mack kept the light steady on the man's foot. "Get your dart rifle. You can have the honors."

King crawled back under the spruce branches and came out with it. He didn't mess around. He held the barrel of the rifle less than a foot away from the motionless man's left heel. He pulled the trigger.

Thfft.

The dart buried itself almost to the feathers.

"Next," King said, and pulled off the other man's boot. He tried to think of something funny to say, the way it would happen in the movies. But how can you say, "Go ahead, make my day," or "*Hasta la vista, baby*" when you are going to shoot the bottom of a man's foot?

So he calmly buried a dart in that man's heel too.

It took both of them to drag first one man and then the other to the base of the rock face. Much easier to drape them with the Mylar space blankets.

They were about to walk away when something beeped under the blanket of the first man.

Mack knelt and lifted the blanket. He found the source of the beep and pulled it loose. The device, about the size of an iPhone, had a screen, and the screen showed four dots.

"Some kind of GPS thing?" Mack asked. "This looks like it's on a map of the island."

"Must be," King answered. "Those dots. Each one is a person, right? Two of us here—and the other set of two dots, moving away from us."

"Perfect," Mack said. "We become dots to replace the two guys we just took out. No way anyone monitoring the thermal sensors can guess that two of those dots are us. Set your GPS to position B and grab your backpack. We'll continue as a pair and make it to the cliff without any problems at all.

King hoped it would be that easy. He wasn't thinking about the cliffs. He was thinking about the other two dots on the tracking device. Each one of those dots representing hunters of men who only had one goal for the night.

Kill. With knives.

CHAPTER 35

Fifteen minutes of walking took them about halfway to the cliffs and nearly all the way to King's death.

Walking, though, wasn't an accurate way to describe it, because that could give the impression that moving through the forbidden zone was like a stroll on city streets. Instead, it was constant motion of ducking beneath branches, balancing on boulders, and finding openings between rock outcrops. All of it was made more difficult by their backpacks. They were guided only by moonlight that disappeared far too often behind drifting clouds. Without the tiny arrow on his GPS to show them the line they needed to take, King would have been lost.

King had let his night vision goggles hang from his neck. He disliked the tunnel vision they gave him, and making sense of the shapes that appeared was difficult because he'd had so little practice.

Mack no longer wore the thermal goggles either. They weren't needed now that King had a device that showed the locations of all heat sources in the forbidden zone. King glanced at it occasionally to reassure himself that the GPS on his wrist was sending Mack and King in the correct direction. The little dots that represented them moving on the map reminded King of the Maps app on an iPhone with a pulsating blue dot that showed the user's location.

King also kept glancing at the thermal dots because he wanted to feel safe from the other two dots. He should have been watching the ground more closely because it suddenly disappeared. And this was how he nearly died.

In actual time, it would have been less than half a second. In terms of sensation, he was in a slow-motion nightmare, frantically flapping his arms to keep his balance, uselessly trying to fly. But in a fight between man and gravity, one inevitably wins and the other inevitably loses.

King dropped. Hard. His gut tightened as he braced for impact, not even knowing where and how he'd fallen, just knowing that there was nothing beneath his feet. At the end of that half second, a giant hand plucked him from the night sky.

At least, that's how it felt.

"King!"

Mack, a few steps behind, had stopped in time.

"Here," King said, his feet dangling, still in total shock and bewilderment.

What had just happened?

Then came the small beam from Mack's flashlight.

It showed a deep and narrow crevice where eons before, part of a rock outcropping had split. King would have landed only a few feet farther down, but on jumbled rocks and rotting tree branches from spruce that had fallen during storms. With luck, he would have only broken some bones. But with broken bones, he would have been unable to travel. And that would have meant death too.

The giant hand that had plucked him from the sky was a spruce that had fallen across the crevice. A broken branch had snagged the straps of his backpack and yanked him as hard as a parachute that had just opened.

"You're okay, right?" Mack said.

"Now that I think about it," King said, "yeah."

All he had to do was wriggle loose from the backpack, ease his way a few feet down to the bottom of the crevice, and then climb out. Even getting across was easy. The fallen spruce formed a natural bridge.

Once they were across the crevice and taking their first steps on the other side, King noticed something far more disturbing than his fall.

"Mack," King said in a low voice. "Could you look at the thermal signatures on this device?"

Mack stopped and shifted the backpack to ease its weight. "Yeah?"

"The two other dots," King said, holding out the device. "They've shifted direction. Before, it seemed like they were drifting away. Now it looks like they're moving toward a position somewhere ahead, between us and the cliffs."

"To cut us off," Mack said. Half question, half statement. "Maybe they had prearranged instructions to meet. Or maybe, somehow, they know we aren't the other two hunters."

"The reason doesn't matter if the result is the same. They can see our location as clearly as we can see them. And they're going to be between us and the cliff."

"Actually it does matter," Mack said. "If it was prearranged, they won't be expecting us instead of the first two, and that might work to our advantage."

King thought about it. "If somehow they know we've switched, they probably think we don't know about them. They can't know we have this tracking device. That's an advantage too, if they believe we don't know they're getting close."

Mack spoke in a dry voice. "So we don't change direction. Because if we do, they'll know we know where they are headed."

Mack's voice became even drier. "That gives us about five minutes to figure out what we're going to do when we meet them."

With no chance of sneaking up on them, King thought. And from a distance, if their enemies were wearing Kevlar and helmets, even less chance of shooting a dart into the small area of exposed skin on their necks.

Then King had an idea.

"Mack," he said. "Remember your MacGyver thing and how you said you had a flare in your backpack to mess with night vision goggles?"

"Yep."

"And remember how the guys we put down said the other two loved using knives too?"

"Trying not to think about it," Mack said.

"But it means they will want to move in close to get us, right?"

"Trying not to think about that either."

"It might work in our favor," King said. "Because maybe we *should* let them come to us. The first reason is that if we stay here and they do head in our direction, it proves that they know we are their targets. And if that's the case, they'll probably assume we won't know they are approaching. I mean, they can't guess we have a thermal location device like they do."

"And the second reason?"

"If they want to move in close instead of shooting us from a distance," King said, "we might have a way to strike back. Let's put it this way, if I had fallen in the crevice, we'd be stopping here to splint a broken ankle or leg, right?"

"Duct tape and pieces of branch," Mack said. "It's not like I'd leave you behind."

"That's how they'd see it too," King said. He outlined his plan.

Hunting humans, King thought, truly was the most dangerous game.

CHAPTER 36

This time, the waiting was easier. Only because waiting the first time had been so difficult.

And this time, King wasn't covered by crinkly Mylar, so he didn't have to keep quite as still. And he wasn't dripping in sweat. Nor was every moment filled with the uncertainty of wondering when the hunters might arrive.

Here, he stood in the open, with his backpack shucked off to the side and short sticks duct taped to his left ankle. He wasn't armed with a dart rifle. Instead, he was leaning on a long stick as if it were a crutch. As he waited, he could glance down at the device and see the approach of two dots, and that took away the uncertainty.

In its place, the only emotion King felt was dread.

Humans were unpredictable. What if King had guessed wrong? What if this pair preferred to shoot, not move in close and use a knife? Or what if this pair liked a combination of both—darts from a distance and then a knife?

The moon came out again, showing his shadow in front of him. There was comfort in seeing Mack's shadow, comfort having his dad at his side. But there was discomfort too because the moonlight made both more visible.

When another cloud put them in darkness, King felt his heart rate slow but only slightly.

King had his night vision goggles on again. Mack didn't need the thermal goggles, not when the handheld device provided them with the information they needed.

The dots on the screen moved closer and closer until it seemed like all four dots had merged. King didn't need the device anymore. He set it down carefully, guessing that the human predators were close enough to hear a sound if he dropped it.

The silence, however, did seem to prove that one of their guesses had been correct. The hunters had not called out, thinking that the thermal images represented their fellow hunters. No, they were moving in as predators.

King strained to see any movement with his night vision goggles. Like before, when it came, it came with ominous slowness, like a stealthy separation of shadows.

"Now," he whispered to Mack.

"Put your weight on it," Mack said. Mack's voice seemed to ring like a bell. There was no doubt it would carry to the hunters, only about 25 steps away. And no doubt that both hunters were observing with night vision goggles.

"It's broken," King answered. He put petulance into the next words. "I don't care how much wrapping you put on it. It's killing me."

"We have to move," Mack said. "We've already wasted too much time standing here. And if there are more of them out there, you really will be dead. Me too. These guys don't mess around. They'll just walk up to us and slaughter us like sheep. We've got nothing left to use to defend ourselves."

"Okay, okay," King said. "Enough. I'm scared as it is."

King remained in a stance that showed his weight on the stick that served as crutch. He shuffled and pretended to half fall and then regain his balance. He made sure to keep track of the green shapes in his goggles, shapes of two human objects moving in closer.

It seemed—and he hoped he wasn't fooling himself—that the hunters were moving with less caution than before.

"Can't do it," King said, making sure his voice was loud and strained. "We might as well get some big rocks and climb in a tree and hope we can catch them by surprise."

"Too late," came a voice. "Time for the four of us to have a party. A pain party."

CHAPTER 37

King wasn't surprised at the sadistic pleasure he heard in the voice that came from the darkness. No different from the first pair. And that had been one of their gambles. That these men enjoyed the chance to hurt and dominate. It meant that they wouldn't shoot darts, but were already in bloodlust, wanting to move in close.

The second man laughed. "That's right, little lambs. *Baa. Baa.* Come to the slaughter."

"Dad!" King said. He pushed off his night vision goggles and let them fall. "Do something."

Those were the code words for King to tell Mack he was ready. And that his eyes were closed.

King heard a scratching sound. Then, with a sudden hissing came a brightness that bloomed through his closed eyelids.

Magnesium flare.

Above the hissing, King heard a scream. Night vision goggles were attuned to pick up and magnify the slightest of lights. For the two hunters, it would have been like having the sun thrust into the center of their brains.

That would buy King and Mack a few moments as the two hunters fought to get some semblance of vision. More importantly, it would look like they were *trying* to buy time.

King dropped the crutch and put one arm around Mack's shoulders. He hopped on his right foot, bending his left leg at the knee to keep the wrapped ankle above the ground.

Together, they did this awkward slow dance to flee the hunters.

Mack had guessed it would take about 90 seconds for their eyes to adjust. He'd also gone back to the crevice and measured about what point they needed to be by the time that 90 seconds ended.

The screams behind them became a string of curses hurled in rage.

Perfect. A raging man is not a thinking man. Whatever bloodlust had been driving those hunters had just increased exponentially.

Mack and King made slow progress. King couldn't get an image out of his mind. He didn't know the bird's name. But when a cat or dog or fox got too close to the bird's nest, it would run in circles, pretending its wing was broken, drawing the animal away from the eggs or hatchlings. Then the bird would time it perfectly, and just as the animal was ready to pounce, it would fly easily out of reach.

Here, a broken ankle would have to do instead of a broken wing. And the timing would need to be equally perfect.

Now each second seemed to be drawn in slow motion. Every one of King's senses was stretched to heightened awareness.

The screams and curses behind them grew louder as both the hunters gained ground with terrifying quickness.

Then came big beams of light. From the hunters behind them. This could be good. Or bad. Good, only if they kept the beams of light on the backs of King and Mack as they fled. Bad if they saw the trap in time.

"Not there yet," Mack said. He didn't need to tell King that everything here was about timing, not losing nerve. "Not there. Not there. Hold steady."

"Dead!" came a shout from behind. Too close behind. "You are dead! Slow dead and so dead!"

The threats were like depth soundings, giving King and Mack precise indications of the narrowing distance. Better yet, they showed the anger that clouded the pursuers' judgment.

Finally, King saw the tiny white beam of Mack's flashlight. Mack had laid the flashlight on the ground so that the beam was parallel to the beginning of the crevice. It told King and Mack exactly where they had to jump.

The magnesium flare kept the hunters behind from being able to see the narrow beam of light. Nor would they see the spruce branches Mack had laid across the gap of the crevice, turning it into a hidden pit.

The shouts and lights were so close that King wanted to risk a peek over his shoulders. When he'd come up with this plan, though, Mack had warned him against looking back if they had flashlights. The entire point was to preserve night vision. If King took a flashlight beam in the eyes, he wouldn't see the tiny sliver of light where Mack's flashlight marked the near edge of the crevice.

"Okay!" Mack said, "Now!"

King dropped his left foot and turned his hopping into a stumbling run. Not enough of a run to raise suspicion in the men behind him, but enough to give him some momentum.

Timing had to be perfect—two steps ahead was the twisted tree with a broken branch leaning into the path. Mack had tightened a rope from the trunk of that tree to a tree on the other side of the path, about a foot high. Low enough that it wouldn't look obvious when King and Mack cleared it with a small jump.

King felt fingers brush across the back of his shoulder. His pursuer! *Now.*

King burst into a full sprint. The tape on his ankle released, and he leaped with power. And then a jump over the rope.

He landed safely on the other side of the rope. A split second later, Mack was beside him.

One step into a full dash. Toward the small beam of light that marked the beginning of the crevice. And then...

Now!

At the sound of a startled shriek behind him, King launched off his front foot and leaped as far forward as he could, wheeling his arms to keep his balance. Olympic broad jumping it wasn't. But it was effective.

He was in the air as he heard more shrieking behind him. And a crashing of branches.

He landed on solid ground on the other side.

Mack thumped down beside him, but the thump was lost in screams of agony.

King had had no chance to witness it, but he could only imagine. He could, however turn to see the results. If he had light.

He fumbled into his back pocket and found Blake's iPhone. King touched a flashlight app.

The covering spruce branches were gone, and the screams in the crevice were turning into moans of agony.

Each of the predators had tripped on the rope, throwing them into the rocks about ten feet below at the bottom of the crevice.

King moved forward and saw both men, crumpled.

On an impulse, King switched the flashlight off and put the iPhone into video mode, with flash.

"Hey down there," King said. "How did the sheep hunt work out for you?"

Mack put a hand on King's arm and spoke quietly. "I'm as tempted as you to taunt them. But when you win, you don't need to do that."

King shook his head in slight amusement. Even now, he was learning from Mack.

"The warden will send out more men," one of the hunters managed to snarl. He was shaved bald, with heavy blue tattooing across his skull and face. Like Spiderman. This was Lassiter. "You'll be dead before the end of the night. And I'm going to spit on your body."

As if to prove it, a walkie-talkie crackled. "Team two, come in. Report."

So that's *why replacing the other two hadn't worked. Walkie-talkies. When they didn't report, the warden realized something was wrong.*

"Let's go," Mack said. "If we move fast, we'll get to the cliff long before another team or two can make it."

"Killdeer," King blurted.

"What?"

Killdeer. Yeah, that was the name of the bird that pretended to be hurt. Killdeer. Strange, how the mind worked.

"Nothing," King said. "I'm ready. Let's go."

CHAPTER 38

At the edge of the cliff, they were out of the trees and exposed. The wind was much stronger, and the crashing of the waves on jagged rocks a hundred feet below had the frightening quality of constant thunder. But the open rock wasn't wide enough to land a chopper. Anyone after them would have to approach on foot. They had time, then. King held a flashlight to guide Mack as Mack assembled lightweight rods of aluminum alloys that he'd taken from his own backpack. Mack wasn't wasting time bolting the frames together. Instead, he was using duct tape, and the ripping sounds of the tape pulling loose from the roll was audible above the wind.

As he had explained, Mack didn't need to bolt the frame together because at most they only needed about 20 yards of outward carry and the 100 feet of drop to the waters of Puget Sound.

Hang gliders. Two of them. From Mack's backpack. The last and final hidden weapon they needed to escape.

Mack worked with the same unhurried efficiency he showed in his woodworking shop. Nothing about him gave an indication that more hunters were undoubtedly in pursuit and that their locations would be clearly indicated by the thermal sensors here at the edge of the forbidden zone.

All they needed was time to get into the water and another five minutes to swim. By then, even when it would be obvious where they'd gone, it would be impossible for helicopter searchlights to find them.

Equally impossible for thermal sensors in a chopper to detect them. The wet suits and rubber hoodies that would protect them from the killing coldness of the water would also hold in their body heat and keep it from betraying their presence. Especially with the snorkels to help them keep their faces and swim masks in the water.

Mack was already working on the frame of the second glider. He had given calm instructions on what King needed to do for a foot launch into the wind. Neither of them were going to strap in with a harness. This was insanely dangerous, but as Mack had pointed out, even if each of them only held on to each crossbar for ten seconds and then dropped, they would have cleared the dangerous rocks and would land in open and deep water, protected from impact by their rubber suits.

"We're good here," Mack said, straightening from his task. "Let's get the decoys in place and put the wings on. To get this far and have the hang gliders blow away while we get the blankets ready would be a real shame."

Decoys.

Mack was referring to a second set of camping blankets that had been stowed in King's backpack. The first had been the Mylar-coated space blankets, meant to reflect heat. Campers also sometimes used heating blankets, powered by 12-volt batteries, with adjustable temperatures. Mack had preset the blanket dial to high, which would get as close as possible to a human body temperature.

Behind them, King and Mack had set up man-sized tripods made of branches lashed together with shoelaces. Now it was time to drape the heat blankets over the tripods and hold the blankets down against the wind by setting heavy rocks on the edges. Mack was confident that these threw off an obvious thermal glow that easily looked like the smudged outline of a human.

Back to the hang glider frames. Mack slipped the nylon wings in place.

He lifted one and handed it toward King. The wing sagged. Mack set it down and grabbed the second one.

"Take this," Mack said. "Looks like one of the frames broke inside the backpack when I bashed the first guy."

"But—"

"Son, not a word."

King had only occasionally heard that tone of voice from Mack, and because Mack used it so infrequently, it had a lot of power.

King took the hang glider from Mack. The wind tugged against it.

He fought the wind, holding the hang glider with one hand and holding the flashlight with the other as Mack unfurled the nylon wing on the other hang glider and found the broken part of the frame. Mack wrapped it with more duct tape.

He grunted with satisfaction. "Yep. We're good."

As he began to put the nylon wing back in place on that half of the glider, both of them froze at a sound that grew above the thunder of the water against rock.

Chopper. Murdoch wasn't sending men in by foot. And just as quickly, Mack unfroze.

"We cut that close," Mack said. "Let's go."

They stood side by side and faced the edge of the cliff, wind plucking at the wings.

"Remember," Mack said. "Five steps, launch, and keep the nose down slightly."

"Got it."

A huge beam of light hit the ground about 200 yards away. Maybe Murdoch wasn't going to drop more men. Maybe he was just going to shoot them at the edge of the cliff, where they were totally exposed.

"No time!" Mack said. "We need to be in the air before we're spotted. If they see the hang glider, all of this was wasted."

King should have known when Mack said *hang glider*, not *hang gliders*.

But he didn't figure that out until later. Just as he didn't figure out till later that Mack had been pretending to fix the broken frame when in reality, no amount of duct tape would have made it possible to fly.

But that was later.

Mack said. "I love you, son. More than life. Always remember that."

And before King could reply, Mack shouted, "Go!"

Mack began to run forward to launch. King matched him stride for stride.

But when they reached the end of the cliff and King soared into the air, there was nobody beside him.

CHAPTER 39

Just like that, King was in the air. Alone. Hanging from aluminum braces of the hang glider. Swooping away from the cliffs.

He looked over his left shoulder for Mack. Then his right shoulder. It was dark, but he should have seen something. Anything.

He turned his head hard to look behind him. And then saw.

A pinprick of light on the cliff's edge. Getting smaller as the hang glider took him away. The light blinked three times. Black. Then blinked three times.

Mack was still on the cliff's edge. Signaling him.

King blinked against tears.

When he looked at the cliff again for the flashlight signal, there was nothing.

Below him, he heard the barking of seals. Even that began to fade as the hang glider took him out into Puget Sound.

Lower and lower until the deep black waters reached up and sucked at the edges of the hang glider and took him into the shock of cold against the skin of his exposed face.

As both wings of the hang glider dragged into the water, King let go of the brace and rolled into the water.

The wet suit gave him buoyancy, and each kick of the flippers moved him with ease through the currents.

He told himself to kick and glide, kick and glide. Not to think. About Mack, left behind on the island. About monsters in the deep. Don't think. Kick and glide.

Every few strokes, he glanced at the glowing GPS on his wrist, following the arrow.

Kick and glide. No thoughts. Kick and glide.

The waves were moderate, and occasionally one would curl and splash into his face, and he would taste salt.

Kick and glide. No thoughts. Kick and glide.

He managed to fall into an illusion of freedom. The floatation effect of the wet suit and the efficiency of the flippers and the endlessness of the water and the rhythm of kick and glide put him in a separate universe where time and gravity didn't exist.

Kick and glide. No thoughts. Kick and glide.

It was like a shock of electricity when the rounded object bumped his belly.

Killer whale, he thought instantly. Then relaxed.

He'd scraped the top of a rock.

Moments later, a crunch of sand took him out of the alternate universe.

He'd made the far shore. With one immediate task. Find the cache of clothing Mack had promised would be waiting at GPS position C.

But, he vowed, that wasn't going to be the end of it.

CHAPTER 40

"Visiting hours are over for the morning," the nurse behind the desk said with tartness in her voice. "Come back after one this afternoon."

King had been out of the water for seven hours. Not even noon, and he felt as if it had been a full day. But then, yes, it had. No sleep during the long night chase and a swim across the strait. The dry clothes that had been waiting for him as Mack had promised had helped, but only slightly. He'd found money as promised but didn't use it to get on a bus. Instead, he'd paid for a taxi driver to take him places, including a military surplus store, where he'd purchased a set of handcuffs that were now hidden in his shirt.

His exhaustion was not only physical but also mental. Worry about what had happened to Mack. Worry about Ella. He was free from the island but only physically.

"I need to see my mom," King told her. "She's in long-term care. Ella King."

The nurse had a middle-age face that had long set into a permanent expression of disapproval, but it softened for King.

For a moment, he thought she was going to deliver the news he'd been dreading. That was part of the mental exhaustion. Remembering how Mack had said they used Ella's condition as a threat, promising something would go wrong if Mack didn't follow orders. King thought she was about to tell him that it was too late, that Ella King had succumbed to her coma, that Ella was...

"I wish I could break the rules for you," the nurse said. "But really, it's only a little more than an hour to wait. We've got kitchen staff going from room to room, and if I break the rules for you, then…"

The nurse gave a helpless shrug.

"Close your eyes, okay?" King said. He wanted to do a happy dance—nothing had happened to his mom! Well, not yet. King couldn't wait an hour. Too many bad things could happen.

The nurse didn't close her eyes. She watched as King walked past the desk and down the hall to where his mom was on a bed, connected to the tubes that kept her alive.

The nurse didn't yell after him to stop. King had guessed right. *She* hadn't broken any rules by giving him permission. So if she didn't say anything, she wouldn't get in trouble. She had enough of a heart to want King to be with his mother.

Of course, King thought, if the nurse knew what he intended to do in the room with those handcuffs, that would have been a different story. Lights would be flashing and horns would be blaring and a full team of security guards would be dashing down the hall to stop him.

At the doorway, King paused. He knew the sight of his mom laying there in helplessness would hammer his heart like an anvil thrown against his chest.

And it did.

King set his jaw hard and walked into the room. Ella had lost weight, and her cheekbones pressed against tight skin. He was glad her hair looked nice. Someone had washed it and brushed it. That was a good sign they were taking care of everything. Especially the stuff that mattered. Like turning her over enough to keep her from getting bedsores. Like exercising her legs and arms.

Her breathing was soft as he leaned in to kiss her cheek.

It reminded him of Mack's story about going into the room when King was a baby to listen to King breathe just so he knew King was alive.

King kissed Ella on the cheek and whispered into her ear. "I love you, Mom. Wake up soon, okay?"

He pulled up a chair to a comfortable position near the bed. He noted with satisfaction that the side bar of the hospital bed formed a railing with a long rectangle. It meant that when he clicked half of the handcuffs around the railing, there was no way to slide them loose.

He locked his wrist into the second half of the handcuffs.

The key was somewhere in a garbage can outside the hospital. Until they brought in a welding unit to cut the side rail of the bed, he was stuck in this room.

King reached into his pocket with his free hand and pulled out Blake's iPhone. He dialed a number that he'd memorized.

When a woman's voice answered, King said, "Hello. I'd like to speak to Warden Murdoch. Please tell him it's the Lyon King."

CHAPTER 41

"King," Murdoch said 30 seconds later, "it's great to hear from you. Things are well?"

What a slime, King thought.

"Better than you must be feeling," King said. He'd told himself to stay cool and collected, but he couldn't help the quick rise of anger and the need to lash out verbally at Murdoch. "Last time I saw you, you smelled like puke. Did that duct tape hurt when they ripped it loose from your eyebrows and mustache?"

Murdoch chuckled. "What a strange thing for you to say. Duct tape? That's what you said, right? Duct tape?"

"So you're pretending I didn't pepper spray you last night? That I didn't use an EID on you? Which, by the way, in case you didn't figure it out, was payback for what you did to Dad."

"I'm trying to follow this conversation," Murdoch said. "But you'll surely agree it seems so random."

"You're denying that you sent prisoners to chase us down?"

"What I'm thinking is that this really is a strange conversation," Murdoch answered.

"I get it," King said. "You think I'm recording this phone call, so you're not going to make any incriminating statements."

"This call just keeps getting stranger. Or are you trying to prank me?"

"Nope," King said. "I want you to release my dad. And I promise your secret will be safe forever."

Murdoch chuckled again. "Yep. Prank."

"If you really thought this was a prank," King said, "you would have hung up by now."

King shifted in his chair. He'd thrown a blanket over the arm that was handcuffed to the bed rail. No sense attracting attention until he needed it.

"No," Murdoch said. "I like you. You're a bright young man. Unless suddenly you've lost your mind, there must be a good reason for this strange phone call. So I'm listening out of genuine curiosity. Go on, please."

"Not much else to say," King answered. "Dad goes free. Nobody touches my mom. Everything is all square. Once they are safe, you are safe."

"I'll humor you. I would be safe from what? But please be careful. If you're going to make some kind of physical threat against me, you'll be breaking a federal law. And by the way, I am recording this conversation. It's standard policy."

Interesting, King thought, for the warden to alert King that the conversation was being recorded. On the recording, if any judge or jury listened to it later in court, it would sound exactly like a friendly warning from Murdoch. On the other hand, it was good way to alert King that because Murdoch knew it was being recorded, Murdoch might say things in a way that King could interpret differently.

"You can be safe from that Macbook Air I took out of the old prison. Blake's Macbook Air. I'm glad he went with a lightweight computer like that. Don't know if I could have made it across Puget Sound with anything heavier. Especially after what it took to make sure water couldn't get inside."

Yeah. It was a bluff.

King continued. "There's enough on that computer to destroy your career. Sorry, I'm wrong about that. Enough on there to destroy your career and put you in prison. That wouldn't be good. Could you imagine what other prisoners in the general population would do to you once they discovered you'd been a prison warden?"

"I'm getting concerned here," Murdoch said.

"You should be." King tried to tamp down his anger.

"What's concerning me is how crazy you sound. I don't know that I can believe this is a prank."

"Three hours," King said. "I've got the Macbook Air with me. You bring my dad to me in three hours, or I call the newspapers and hand over the computer."

"I'm getting even more concerned here."

King wondered if Murdoch was using double-speak. Because Murdoch had warned King that the call was being recorded, he could later claim he meant he was concerned about King. But right now, he might actually be admitting he was really concerned about King's threat.

So King played it that way.

"What I'm thinking," King said, "is that somehow you have a way to track where the phone call is coming from. If I had been afraid of that, I would have hung up a long time ago. But I've got the Macbook Air, and I'm going to hide it between now and when you come visit. Even if you order someone right now to come get me, I'll have plenty of time to hide it. So I'm not afraid to tell you where I am. Besides you need to know in order to bring me my dad. Are you listening?"

"Only because I'm concerned about your craziness here."

"I'm at the hospital. In my mom's room. After we hang up, I'm going to put the Macbook Air in a place you'll never find. And then I'm going to return to her room and handcuff myself to her bed. So if you or some goon arrives, it's going to cause a big fuss if you try to take me away. But you're smarter than that, right? Bring my dad. Then you're safe."

"King, King, King," Murdoch sighed. "I think I'm going to need to talk to your dad about this. It's his day off, so I'll give him a call at home and tell him that you've really crossed a line here."

Brief silence.

"Hang on," Murdoch said. "How about you call your dad first? Then call me back, and I'll let you apologize for this phone call."

"Three hours," King said.

King pulled the phone away from his ear and used his thumb on the touch screen to end the call.

CHAPTER 42

King's arm was sore. With his one wrist handcuffed to the bed railing, he couldn't move much as he spoke on the phone. Nor, of course, could he shift the phone from one hand to another as people often did during long phone calls.

He stretched his free arm, and then, after a few hesitant seconds, King dialed another number and put the cell phone back to his ear. He was shocked when someone answered the cell phone on the other end.

"Dad?" King said.

"Hey," Mack said. "Sorry I missed you for breakfast. You still at MJ's working on a project?"

"I wasn't at MJ's," King said. "You know that."

"That's what your note said. I found it on the breakfast table this morning."

Only one conclusion to draw here, King told himself. Mack was under guard. This call was being recorded too.

"So you're at home," King said.

"Where else? Murdoch called before I started my day shift. Gave me the day off."

"Sure," King said. "And you're alone."

"King, if I didn't have a headache, this might be a little easier to deal with. But just so you know, my brain feels swollen. Been drinking lots of water too. Crazy thirsty. So I'm not in the best of moods."

"What about last night?" King asked.

"Last night?"

This was seriously starting to make King mad. He wasn't going to let Murdoch win this round.

"Mack," he said. "You know where Mom's iPhone is, right?"

"Yeah, unless you moved it."

With Ella in the hospital, they'd left everything at home as it was in her pottery workshop. To change things would be to admit defeat, to say that they had given up hope of her ever coming out of the coma.

"I know you're not a big fan of technology," King said, "but I need you to do me a huge favor. Can you get the phone and turn it on? There's a button on the top right. Press and hold down until a white apple appears on the screen."

"This headache is irritating me," Mack said.

"It's important to me," King answered. He was not going to let Mack wiggle out of this. He could picture Mack in a room somewhere in the SCC with guards watching him. Or Murdoch staring down at him, making sure Mack didn't say anything to let King know where Mack was.

"Okay." Mack sighed.

"Don't hang up with your phone," King said. Mack's cell phone was about ten years old. A stray thought hit King. Weird, in this moment, wondering about the phrase he had just used. *Don't hang up the phone*. Nobody hung up cell phones anymore. That was from before, when the receiver was on a hook and you lifted up the receiver and took it off the hook to make a call. Well, maybe that's why the thought hit King. Because of how old his dad's cell phone was. And how his dad's technological world was back in the "hang up the phone" days.

"No way am I hanging up," Mack said with some humor back in his voice. "If you want me on your mom's iPhone, I'm going to have to stay on this one for instructions."

"Exactly," King said.

Silence. King imagined Mack looking at the warden with a "Now what?" expression. How could Mack go to the pottery workshop and get Ella's iPhone when Mack was stuck in some cell pretending to be in the house?

While King was waiting, the door to the hospital room opened. An orderly walked in with a gadget. A big guy, dark hair, bearded. With shoulders stretching the green uniform tight and a chest that seemed ready to bust open the fabric.

King was glad he had a blanket hiding the handcuffs. He wasn't ready yet for the questions that would happen when someone noticed. "I'm her son," King explained.

The orderly answered. "Need to check her temperature."

King shrugged and held out the phone briefly, so that the orderly could see King wasn't interested in a conversation. King wanted the guy out of here as soon as possible.

The orderly went to the other side of the bed and touched the gadget against Ella's skull. There was an almost inaudible beep.

The orderly checked a screen on the gadget and gave King a thumbs up.

Then the guy tapped some of the drip tubes and gave a nod.

After that, he walked out, just as Mack spoke again into King's ear. "Okay. Believe it or not, I actually figured out how to turn it on. The little white apple is there."

"Sure," King said. Sarcastic.

"You don't need to speak to me like I'm a child." Mack snorted. "Well, actually, when it comes to this, you probably do."

"Okay," King said, knowing Murdoch wasn't going to be able to keep this charade going much longer. "Tell me when the home screen appears."

"Home screen?"

"When the apple goes away and the photo shows up. Of the two of us sitting on a dock."

"Oh." Ten seconds passed. "Now. But that's not the photo. It's one of you when you were about five years old. In a cowboy outfit."

"She must have changed it," King said. He was impressed that his dad could remember which photo had been on the home screen. King had deliberately mentioned a different photo as a test. If Mack had agreed the dock photo was on the screen, the game would have been over. But King wasn't through with this. He'd prove Murdoch wrong and then call Murdoch again and shorten the deadline to two hours.

"So," King said. "I'm about to end this call on my end. Then I'm going to call you on Mom's iPhone using FaceTime."

"You mean that thing where you can talk to each other on video, right? That's so Dick Tracey to me."

"Huh?" King said.

"Dick Tracey." Short pause. "Sorry. See, this shows how much things have changed since I was a kid. Dick Tracy was a comic book detective set in the future. He had a wristwatch that he used to make phone calls. Video calls too. It was cool to us as kids, but nobody really believed or expected it would ever happen."

"Yeah," King said. "Like your MacGyver guy?"

"MacGyver. I'm impressed you know about MacGyver. My favorite show when I was a kid."

Mack's acting was good, pretending last night's conversation hadn't happened.

King went along with it. "Dick Tracy. Okay, I'm about to Dick Tracy you. Just watch the screen and hit Accept, and then we'll be connected."

"Why are we doing all this?" Mack said. "You could just walk over here from MJ's house."

"Part of my project," King said. "How's that?"

"Go for it," Mack said. "But if I mess up, call me back on my cell."

Oh, King thought. That's how they are going to play it. Pretend that Mack doesn't know how to accept an incoming FaceTime request.

Still, King just realized he'd lost this game. He'd hit FaceTime, Mack wouldn't answer because he couldn't answer where he was in a prison cell, King would have to call back to Mack's cell, and Mack would apologize for getting the technology wrong, and King would be no closer to proving to Murdoch that he knew Murdoch was holding Mack as a hostage. It's probably why Murdoch had allowed Mack to have his cell phone. So Mack could answer anyone who called and pretend everything was okay.

King wasn't too upset about this. He was just glad Mack was still alive. Murdoch was in a tight place and would have to do something before the three-hour deadline was over.

Then King tried to remember. What kind of signal shows that you're trying to FaceTime someone when his iPhone is shut off? Does it show unavailable, or does it try to ring through until you give up and end the attempt?

One way to find out.

"Well," he said to Mack. "Here goes. I'm about to end the call on your cell. Hopefully you'll figure out how to answer on Mom's iPhone."

It took King about ten seconds to put his Mom's cell number into the iPhone he was using, which was the one he'd found in a tree that started all of this.

When that was ready, King made the FaceTime attempt. And was startled when Mack's face appeared on the screen.

"What?" King said. "It's you. You've got her phone?"

"Well, you made me do it," Mack said.

"How's the battery level?" King asked. "Top of screen. Little battery symbol."

"Red," Mack said. "I'm going to guess that's not good."

"No," King answered. "We'll have to talk fast." *If you're really holding Mom's iPhone.*

Mack peered at the screen, something obvious through the video. "Where are you? That doesn't look like MJ's house."

King fought his confusion. His dad had pushed King off a cliff the night before. With King in a hang glider. Wearing a wet suit and flippers. How could Mack actually expect that King was at MJ's house?

"Look at the top of the screen," King said. He was watching his own iPhone screen so he knew he was describing it accurately. "There's a symbol of an arrow chasing another arrow. If you touch that symbol, the phone will switch to the rear camera."

"Rear? This thing has two cameras? Mack shook his head, a movement clear in the video conversation. "Dick Tracey had nothing on this."

King saw his dad's finger approach the screen and then saw the transition. And unbelievably, he saw some of the unfinished pottery that Ella had been working on before the coma.

"Mack," King said. "Can you turn in a circle and show me all of the room?"

"Must be some weird project you are working on with MJ," Mack said.

On his own iPhone, King saw the panoramic view of his mom's pottery room as Mack made a slow circle. All 360 degrees.

This was insane. What was going on? Murdoch had actually sent Mack back to the house after capturing him?

But why?

Maybe Murdoch had kept using the threat of hurting Ella as a way to force Mack to pretend nothing had happened. Maybe Murdoch figured that was easier than holding Mack hostage. However, if Mack truly was alone—and it looked like he was—Mack would be able to speak the truth.

"Hey," King said. "Can you hit the reverse button again so I can see you?"

"Sure. This is easy. Maybe I should get one of these things."

His dad's face appeared in the screen again.

"Mack," King said. "You're alone in the house, right?"

"Already told you that." Mack's expression seemed genuinely puzzled.

"So you can talk freely."

Mack frowned. "Of course."

"Then tell me this," King said. "How did you escape the guys who were chasing us last night through the forbidden zone?"

Mack's frown deepened. "Son, I truly have no idea what you're talking about. Can you help me out on this?"

The screen went black.

Mack had been using Ella's iPhone. The battery was nearly dead. And it seemed Mack had no idea of what had happened the night before.

Or Mack was lying because somehow he was part of it and had decided to hang up to avoid more questions.

Nothing made sense to King.

There was only one thing to do.

Wait. Handcuffed to his mom's hospital bed. With the key to the handcuffs discarded in a dumpster, far out of his reach.

CHAPTER 43

Five minutes passed with King listening to the slow rise and fall of Ella's breathing.

It occurred to him that since walking outside of the old prison building the night before, this was the first time he could slow down and let his mind wander. He couldn't describe it as his first moment to relax. No way was he relaxed. He felt like a guitar string just before the last turn of the tuning peg snapped it.

But since walking out of the old prison building, he had constantly been on the move, focused and living in each moment. From pepper spraying the warden, to the terror of the pursuit on the island, to the determined stroke after stroke to get him across the sound, to his checklist of tasks since arriving on the mainland to be ready for whatever happened here in the hospital.

King allowed himself to become aware of his own breathing. The rise and fall of his own chest. He didn't like this, the time to think.

Because then he would have to wonder about the strange conversation with his father and all that it might imply. Maybe, somehow, Mack really was part of some of this. The money in his account, the surveillance tapes, the…

King ordered himself to stop thinking. He focused on breathing.

But that only reminded him of the helplessness of his mother. Near enough that he could reach out and brush away some of the hair that had fallen across her forehead. Yet so achingly far away.

And again her breathing reminded him of how Mack had described going into King's room when King was a baby just to listen and be reassured.

It took King a second to realize that tears were rolling down his cheek. Could have been the stress. A reaction to exhaustion. But King knew the truth. It was the realization of how much he loved Mack and Ella, and how it hurt that it all seemed to have been destroyed. How much his love and respect for Mack meant to him, and how much he was afraid that what he was doing now would lead to an awful discovery that Mack was not the person he appeared to be since King's first memory of reaching up for Mack's hand.

As he wiped away the tears with his free hand, the big, dark-bearded orderly entered the room again.

"Sorry," the orderly said. Soft, like he meant it. "Need to adjust the bed."

A hospital tag showed his name. Jerome Claridon.

He almost brushed King, passing close to King's chair. King, of course, couldn't move. Not without exposing the set of handcuffs hidden beneath the blanket. It still wasn't time for anyone to learn about the handcuffs.

Jerome was standing directly behind King's chair.

King heard the whine of an electric engine and saw the part of the bed beneath his mother's upper body adjust at an upward angle.

Then he felt a sting in the meat of his right shoulder.

He spun his head.

There was a hand on his shoulder, the big hand of the orderly. With a hypodermic needle held expertly in the large fingers.

The other hand shot down to King's upper arm.

"Hold steady," Jerome said. "You don't want to break the needle off in your arm."

King was helpless. His hand handcuffed to the bed. He reached up with his right hand toward his right shoulder but had no leverage.

It didn't matter anyway.

Jerome pulled the hypo loose.

"We're going to go for a walk," Jerome said. "Don't fight me on this, or your mother will pay for it."

King winced. He wished his left hand was free so he could reach across and rub his right shoulder. But he was glad his left hand wasn't free. Because he wasn't going to go for a walk.

"Staying," King said. He pulled off the blanket, exposing the set of handcuffs that secured him to the bed railing. "And going to yell for help, so don't…"

What he wanted to say was *Don't do anything to Ella.*

But what came out seemed to be slow motion babble. Strange, he thought. His brain was telling his mouth what to say, but his mouth wouldn't follow directions.

He watched in fascination—as if he were having an out-of-body experience—while the big orderly stepped in front of him and pulled out a pair of bolt cutters that he'd hidden in his shirt behind his back, just as King had hidden the handcuffs.

Wow, King thought. *Bolt cutters. Cool. The handles are long enough to give amazing leverage. Wow. A person could shear right though chain links with it.*

Wow. And cool, King thought. *Look at the orderly reach out to cut the handcuff links.*

Hang on, King thought. *If he does that, I won't be handcuffed any-more. That's not good, right?*

In horrible slow motion, he tried to twist and struggle with his left hand, bucking his wrist up and down to avoid the blades of the cutters.

Wow. And cool, King thought. *My hand isn't moving. My brain is tell-ing my hand to move, but my hand isn't listening.* He was amazed that he felt so rubbery and weak.

Wow. And cool, King thought. *Look at that. The handcuff is snapped in two.*

"Come on," Jerome said, reaching down to grasp King by his right elbow and lifting him out of the chair. "Time to go."

Wow. And cool, King thought. *Look at me. I'm walking. With this Jerome dude.*

Then he began to lose conscious thought. It seemed like the ending of a movie, where the outer edges of the screen turn black and the black fills in more and more until there's only a little circle remaining in the cen-ter that's not black anymore, and then even that little circle disappears.

CHAPTER 44

Strictly speaking, King didn't wake from unconsciousness. Instead, he gradually became aware of his surroundings, of the sounds and smells and a vibration and humming that took him a long time to understand.

He was thirsty, the interior of his mouth puckered as if he had been sucking on sand.

He was laying on a piece of loose carpet in the back of a cargo van. No windows. Just ribbed walls of bare sheet metal. It smelled like paint, and splashes of various colors against the walls confirmed the cargo van's previous use. The van now had a different mission, King thought grimly, as he tried to shift into a comfortable position on the carpet. He was a slab of meat, hands and feet bound. He glanced down at his ankles and saw the white adhesive tape that medical people used to hold gauze in place over wounds. Made sense, if he'd been taken away by the orderly. He couldn't tell. He was unable to see the driver because of a half wall directly behind the driver's seat.

He was unable to see his hands. They were behind his back, and every bump hurt because of the tension it put against his shoulders.

The bumps and vibration were from the movement of the cargo van. An abrasive humming sound gave King an indication of the speed of the vehicle. Highway speed. He was moving a mile a minute away from the hospital.

King had no idea how long he'd been in the twilight zone of whatever pharmaceutical had been injected into his shoulder.

The fact that he had not been blindfolded worried King. A lot. It meant whoever was using this cargo van to transport a bound human instead of cans of paint really didn't care what the human witnessed.

If that were the case, King could think of nothing good that was ahead of him. Not caring if there *was* a witness indicated you also didn't care *for* the witness. Because the witness wasn't going to be a witness for long.

King looked for anything that might be sharp enough to cut at the edge of the tape on his wrists. He wanted to see a sheet-metal screw sticking out from the wall or floor of the cargo van.

He told himself he wasn't going to become a dead witness without a fight.

*

Maybe a half hour later, the van rolled to a stop. From his position, King still couldn't see the driver. But he heard the driver's door open and close. He heard footsteps as the driver walked around the van. That told King they were on hard ground. Asphalt parking lot maybe.

The rear van door opened. King had expected that. He kept his eyes closed. He had not had any luck finding something sharp to cut through the adhesive tape. Maybe he could try the element of surprise.

He waited until he sensed a shadow and then kicked upward as hard as he could. His feet met no resistance.

"Think I'm stupid?" It was the orderly's voice.

King opened his eyes, and the brightness hurt. Beyond the orderly's shoulders, he caught a glimpse of snowy mountain peaks. They'd moved a long way from Tacoma.

The large man rolled King over. "Don't kick, okay? I'll just have to hurt you."

King kicked anyway. He wasn't going to be a passive victim, and everything about the situation told him he was going to get hurt one way or another.

Something thumped his head. A fist. Jerome's fist.

"Enough," Jerome said.

"Why are you doing this?" King asked.

"Don't know," Jerome said. "Don't care. I just listen to a voice on the other end of the phone."

"Where are we going?"

"Don't ask. You really don't want to know, okay?"

"Not okay," King said.

"Whatever." The orderly began to drag King out of the van. King thumped around, trying to make it difficult for the orderly.

Another thump on the head made King see spots.

"You can walk," Jerome said, "or I can give you another needle."

"Of what?" King wanted the orderly to talk. About anything.

"Of whatever. It works, that's all you need to know."

The utter lack of care in the orderly's voice frightened King. This process of taking another human in a cargo van, as if the human were cargo, was obviously just a job to the orderly.

"Tell me one thing," King said, "and I promise I won't struggle. Who sent you?"

The orderly succeeded in yanking King out of the van. King landed on his feet. With the tape securing his legs together so tightly that his ankles touched, he could barely keep his balance.

The orderly spun King away from the van and stepped behind him. It gave King a clear view of where they were. In a parking lot at the base of a hiking trail. Not good. Definitely not good.

"Don't know who pays the bills," Jerome said. "That's a truthful answer. So you owe me to deliver on your promise. I really don't want to carry you."

"Where?" King asked.

Something dropped over his neck from behind. It felt cold. Seconds later, there was a jolt of tightness that seemed to fracture his Adam's apple.

"In case you can't figure it out," the orderly said, "that's a choke chain. Works on dogs. It'll work on you."

There was a slight ripping sound at his ankles. Behind him, the orderly must have squatted and cut the tape loose, because King could move his legs. He staggered slightly, keeping his balance as he spread his legs.

"Now we walk," Jerome said.

King felt a jab in his back.

"Yep," Jerome said. "A knife. Don't be stupid, okay? I've got a short grip on this choke chain and a tight grip on my knife. The only place you're going is where I want you to go."

That's when a cell phone rang.

CHAPTER 45

"Yeah," Jerome said into the phone.

A pause.

"Yeah," Jerome said again. "We're here."

Another pause.

Then Jerome said to King, "It's for you."

King was hoping Jerome would cut the tape on King's wrists so King could hold the phone.

Nope.

"I've got Blake's computer." A robotic voice reached King from the back of his skull. He realized that Jerome had put the cell on speaker mode and was holding it right behind King at head level. The robotic voice was some kind of computer-simulation that made it impossible to recognize. "Had it at dawn long before you called from the hospital. All it took was bloodhounds and a metal detector. Just wanted you to know that your bluff didn't work. You have nothing. Understand? Nothing. That's why you're headed into the mountains. Everyone knows you wanted off the island. When you don't come back, you'll be a runaway who just disappeared. Like tens of thousands of others every year."

"Hey," Jerome said to the cell-phone voice. "Thanks. You know how hard it's going to be to move him now that he knows?"

"He was smart enough to know it all along," the computer voice said in garbled tones. "That's why he handcuffed himself to a bed. Now get it done. Even if you have to drag him to the edge of the cliff. Then go back to the hospital."

Click. The call ended.

Jerome sighed. "Guess it's time for a needle. Probably for the best. You won't know what hit you."

"And neither will you," King said.

Jerome jerked on the choke chain. "Give it up. Don't bother."

"Armageddon," King said.

"Huh?"

"Armageddon. It's a code word."

"It's a stupid code word. Doesn't mean a thing to me."

"Not yet," King said.

King waited. When nothing happened, he felt a sick clunking in his stomach. He'd put too much faith in the promises that had been made to him a few hours earlier in an office in downtown Seattle.

"Armageddon," King repeated.

The promises. From a man in a navy blue suit with cropped hair and a face that showed no expression and who had nearly black eyes darker than the skin of the man's face, eyes that had focused on King with an intensity that was more fascinating than frightening.

"Yes, you're going to be like a goat tethered to a stake to bring in the tiger. But the tiger won't make it to the goat. Because we'll be there. If you're in a tight situation, talk long enough for us to get a sense of what is happening and get our men into position. No matter where you are, we'll be there. We've got choppers. We've got a small army. We're the best, the elite. We know how to hunt men."

But what if the transmitter sewn into his jacket had failed? What if somehow choppers had lost the van? What if the best of the best CIA agents weren't good enough?

"Armageddon," King tried again.

"Don't get on my nerves," Jerome said. "Wait. Too late. You already are. Maybe I won't give you a needle. The choke chain will do it."

As if to prove it, Jerome gave another yank, and King staggered.

King said it again, as calmly as he could, given the massive amount of adrenalin that was beginning to surge through his body.

Where were the best of the best? The man hunters?

King hadn't known what to expect when it arrived. Only that he'd been promised, no matter what, that it would arrive.

And finally it did.

Thfft. Thfft.

The sound didn't mean anything to King at first. But it must have meant something to Jerome because King heard the big man grunt.

King turned slightly. Saw surprise on Jerome's face and two darts sticking out of the side of Jerome's neck.

As Jerome sagged to his knees in blank incomprehension, from 30 feet away, two men in camo stepped out of the bushes.

A lot of things to say ran through King's mind. *Took you long enough. Good to see you. Nice shooting.*

Instead, he moved out of the way so that Jerome hit the ground instead of King.

King knew it was going to feel good to get that choke chain off his neck.

CHAPTER 46

Inside a commuter helicopter, King waited for the blades to slow to a stop shortly after it had settled on a helipad.

"We're in Fort Lewis," King said to the pilot, a man in a navy blue suit with cropped hair and a face that showed no expression and who had near black eyes darker than the skin of the man's face. His name was Evans. No first name. Just Evans. "A military base."

"To be accurate," Evans answered, "it's Joint Base Lewis-McChord."

Back at the parking lot near the old van where King had been held prisoner, two choppers had landed shortly after the two-person team had taken Jerome down with darts. One of the choppers had been large enough for six men and a couple of women to step down and begin processing the scene. The second chopper, much smaller, was lightweight and looked like a traffic chopper that television stations in Seattle used. This was the one that Evans piloted, and after King had boarded, Evans had taken them west to the urban sprawl of Seattle and Tacoma.

Joint Base Lewis-McChord had been an easy guess for King. On the approach, King had been able to see McNeil Island across Puget Sound. And things were starting to make more sense. If Evans was based out of Fort Lewis, that explained how he'd arrived so quickly at the FBI office in Seattle earlier that morning. And if the special units that Evans commanded were based out of Fort Lewis, it also explained how he'd been able to pull the operation together so quickly.

"Here's my question," King said to Evans. "Is the US government willing to kill its own citizens to protect this secret?"

The chopper was completely silent, and no military personnel had approached it. Obviously, it had been cleared to land, and Evans was expected.

"Before I answer that," Evans said, "I will tell you what's been happening on the island. As you know, I'm CIA, and we have been running secret night games on the island to train our special ops group. It's no coincidence that I'm based out of JBLM. This is also the home base for the 201st Battlefield Surveillance Brigade. The island provides training for some of their soldiers too. McNeil Island is the perfect location for all of our needs."

"Training," King repeated.

"We started this about a year ago. Murdoch is CIA, and he's in control of the prison and the situation on the island. In these games, unlike training games the military runs elsewhere, our operatives had to pit themselves against dangerous felons in situations where if they lost, they faced real risks. For further clarity, in case you were unaware of what *is* public knowledge, Special Operations Group agents—SOG's—are drawn from the elite of the elite. The army, for example, has the Delta Force. The navy has something called DEVGRU, but you probably know it as SEAL Team Six. The air force equivalent is the 24th Special Tactics Squadron. We take only the top 5 percent from each of those special forces for our own. The task is simple. Go places where we need them and do things no other soldiers could accomplish."

He paused. "And sometimes they need to hunt other men."

He waited to see if there would be a protest. "Bin Laden, for example. Other terrorists. Some known to the world. Some not. You can debate the morality of this, but the fact is that without it, America would be less safe. SOG tactics and operations are highly secret, but as an arm of the CIA, the mission of the SOG is a matter of public record."

"I'm not here to debate," King said. "I want to understand what's been happening."

"We've learned that regardless of how well we train our operatives," Evans answered, "90 percent of failures or casualties occur within the first three missions. Once an operative makes it past that threshold, he's likely to succeed and return alive. What we needed—and found here on the island—was a real-life situation that dropped the failure rate during the first three missions significantly. Forcing them to hunt and be hunted by dangerous humans in training sessions on McNeil Island is an extremely practical way to prepare for other missions."

Evans looked past King with a thousand-yard stare, as if recalling a dangerous mission. Then he focused his laser eyes back on King. "As a secondary benefit, we've used this as a way to test a new drug that erases short-term memory and helps prevent posttraumatic stress disorders all across the military. It's a variation of something called metyrapone."

"Is that what Jerome used on me?"

Evans shook his head negative. "Our drug is injected after the hunt, not before or during. What he used on you was something to make you compliant. My best guess is flunitrazepam. It's easy to obtain at a hospital. It's a hypnotic sedative and skeletal muscle relaxant." Evans smiled grimly. "And yes, we've used it too on occasion. For the same purpose he did."

"On the phone, my dad couldn't remember anything from last night," King said. Every word had been recorded because the CIA had been in on this from the moment in the Seattle office when King had used cell phone video to convince Evans that King knew about the night hunts on McNeil Island. Mack had sent King straight to the FBI office. And about 20 minutes after King arrived there, Evans had walked in, and the CIA had taken over the operation.

"Easy conclusion," Evans said. "Murdoch has full knowledge of metyrapone. Your father might remember a few fragments but only if you tell him what happened."

The answer lifted a burden from King. It didn't explain the quarter million dollars in the bank account, but it meant Mack had not been acting during the FaceTime call. Mack hadn't been working with Murdoch.

Evans said, "Our variation of metyrapone has the potential to help a lot of soldiers. If they are injected right after a traumatic battle, it saves them a tremendous amount of stress and could ease their transition back to civilian life. So the island provided us a situation where the most ruthless criminals in America were locked away forever. We could put them in real-life hunting situations and then test the effectiveness of the drug following each hunt. Few remember that they've hunted our men. Or that they've been hunted and shot with darts."

"Some people might call that monstrous," King said.

"Yes," Evans said calmly. "And then again, many others of us have 9/11 seared in our memories and are determined not to allow it to happen again. I suggest you remember your earlier statement that now is not the time or place to debate it. You will have decisions to make shortly, and I want you to have as much knowledge as possible as I answer your question as to whether the US government is willing to kill its own citizens if necessary to protect this secret."

CHAPTER 47

"Everything so far indicates that what you brought me earlier is accurate, and that video you shot of the prisoner with the Spiderman face is the last bit of proof I needed," Evans said to King. "And we owe you a debt for that. We were unaware that Murdoch had gone renegade on us and was taking advantage of this situation to bring in private trophy hunters who paid huge bounties to hunt the most dangerous predator in the world."

Evans leaned back in his pilot's chair and looked ahead through the bubble of the chopper window. "In retrospect, it's something that could be too tempting for the wrong person. Internet forums make it easy to stay anonymous as you look for wealthy clients. And you easily could keep the location of the island secret too. Say the client is from Texas. You'd just need to make sure he doesn't have any GPS technology, put him on an airplane at night, land at a private airport somewhere on the mainland, and keep him blindfolded during the final chopper flight to the island.

King couldn't help but think about the money hidden in Mack's bank account. He'd been afraid to ask Mack about it the night of the escape. And King sure wasn't going to bring it up now in front of the CIA.

"We had a deal," Evans said, shifting the conversation abruptly, "I've delivered on everything you wanted, so now I want my payment. Answers. How did you find out about Murdoch?"

"Dead Man's Switch," King said.

Evans raised an eyebrow as a question mark.

"It's a website. You set up a bunch of emails to go out if you don't put in a password every day. That's how I got the first email from Blake Watt. Blake's funeral was a few weeks ago. Blake's the one who found out. Blake's emails started coming out and led me along little by little. The final proof is all on the Macbook Air that Murdoch has."

"A website that sends out info?" Evans glared at King. "You told me you could keep this secret. So now some website is out there holding all this information that could explode on the world at any time?"

"I didn't lie," King said. "We can keep it secret."

King glanced at his watch. He'd already plugged in the password for the day and had bought another 24 hours, but Evans wouldn't know this. Best thing to do here would be to squeeze Evans with time pressure the way that Blake had squeezed King.

"We have about four hours to stop the release of the info," King said. "But not until you come up with some guarantee that nothing will happen to me or my dad or my friend MJ. You know, that part about whether we believe the CIA would kill American citizens to keep a secret."

Evans nodded, but none of the sudden anger left his face. "Releasing that information would be something we'd hate to see. We want the lowest profile possible, which is why I'd much rather work with you to keep it secret than work against you if you went to the press. But if you did go to the newspapers right now with your story, the CIA would find a way to deny any plausibility. It's the Internet age. People make wild claims all the time."

Evans snorted. "If you took this public, we could arrest you and charge you with one thing or another under the Homeland Security Act. But we wouldn't, because if we did, that would be an indication that there was truth behind the accusations. No, we'd just let the rumors continue and start our own whisper campaign against the accusers. Stories about your backgrounds would be leaked to the press, and those stories would be outrageously false but put you in a bad light."

Evans smiled grimly. "Your mother, for example, would be exposed for her time with bikers as she sold meth and marijuana to underage kids in bars."

King began to arch his back in indignation. "She did not."

"Of course not," Evans said. "But we'd find ways to get into court-house computers and make it look as if she had a jail record. I promise you right now, if you went public with this, it would be far worse for each of your parents' reputations than for the reputation of the CIA. Their credit scores would be destroyed; they'd be out of work. And all that you would have inflicted on us is yet another conspiracy theory."

"That's what I needed to hear," King said. "Now I know I can trust you."

"What, bringing an elite force of special operatives to rescue you wasn't enough?"

"No," King said. "You didn't do that for me. You did it because of Murdoch. He was playing you like a fool and making millions because of it. You didn't do me a favor. I did you one by bringing this to you."

Evans grunted but didn't agree or disagree.

King tossed his iPhone to Evans, who caught it with a fluid ath-letic movement.

"Dead Man's Switch," King said. "It's not only a website. It's also a game app."

Evans hit the home button and glanced down. "Password?"

"Two eight five five."

Evans unlocked the phone.

"Look through it," King told Evans. "Check out the apps."

After about 30 seconds, Evans said, "Hundreds."

"Actually, 3520, if you want to be exact," King said. "It's Blake Watt's phone. All those games and apps made no sense. Then I thought about how easy it would be to hide an app in there. So I did a search. Try it. You know how to go to the search screen? Go to—"

"You kids think you're the only ones who understand technology."

"You there?"

"Give me a second," Evans said.

"Just—"

King stopped when Evans shot him a cold glare. Then King grinned, letting Evans know King was messing with him.

"Do a search for Dead Man's Switch," King said.

Evans worked his thumb on the screen. Then lowered his eyebrows as the result came up. "Game app. And don't tell me. Tap it and it will open."

King waited. He was silent as he watched Evans, whose eyes widened moments later.

"It's on an island. CIA operatives. Each given different weapons. Hunting. This is…this is…"

Evans was speechless.

"It's ninety-nine cents, is what is," King said. "Available on iTunes."

"We'll get it pulled," Evans said.

"Come on," King said. "Who would believe something that crazy?"

"Ha, ha," Evans said. Short pause. "What's your point here?"

"Blake Watt was a computer wizard. He's the one who created it. I know that because I looked up the game app developer. He calls it DMS Apps. It's proof Blake also knew about the CIA hunting games on the island."

"And?"

"Everything he pointed us to was meant to expose Murdoch. Yet if Blake also knew about the CIA, that means I wondered if maybe the CIA knew about Blake too. If his drowning wasn't an accident. That led me to the big question. Who got rid of Blake? Murdoch? Or you guys?"

Evans folded his arms. "Do I really have to answer? We rescued you."

"Maybe some kind of reverse thing. Making it look like you're against Murdoch to get me to tell you what I know. After all, you admitted Murdoch is CIA as well."

"*Was* CIA. In about an hour, his career is finished. It's a short hop to the island from here."

"I didn't know who to trust until now. The CIA doesn't need to get rid of people to keep it secret. You can use other methods."

"I still don't understand your point."

"It's this," King said. "You didn't need to kidnap Blake. You would have threatened him and his parents just like you threatened me. That means you didn't kidnap Blake, it meant Murdoch did."

"Kidnap? He's the kid who drowned."

"Unless Murdoch took him and Blake was smart enough to threaten

Murdoch with exposure with the dead man's switch so that Murdoch couldn't just kill him," King said. "And if Murdoch kidnapped Blake, I'll bet he's still on the island. Alive and waiting for us to do something about it."

King glanced at his watch. "We've got under four hours to find him before the next emails go out to the entire media."

"Now?" Evans exploded. "Now you tell me this? Not this morning when you first came to my office. But now?"

King shrugged. "Had to be sure about you."

"Four hours. You wait to tell me we've got an entire island to search for the kid, and you wait until there's four hours left to announce this? Let me tell you, if this hits the Internet, all of you are going to be miserable for the rest of your lives. His family. Your family. The other kid's family. What's his name. M something.

"MJ."

"Four hours until the dead man's switch is triggered. You have no idea how angry I am, and no idea how bad that is for you."

"We don't need four hours," King said. "Can you think of a better place to keep a kid imprisoned than in an actual prison?"

CHAPTER 48

"Hop aboard," Evans said to Warden Murdoch. Evans was standing alone on the helicopter deck, door open and looking down at the warden. "We need to talk."

"Aboard" meant the platform of the UH-1 gunship. Evans had called it a Huey. It was big enough to conceal the entire commando unit. Five minutes before, it had thumped down from the sky, landing on the island's helipad. King had seen none of the view of Puget Sound on the ten-minute flight from Fort Lewis. He was tucked in the back, feeling tiny among a dozen SOG men inside the chopper in their full combat gear, including helmets. The Huey's blades—long scythes that cut the air with frightening efficiency—had been slowing since landing and had made a final rotation when Murdoch had appeared, driving up in his shiny black Jeep TJ. King recognized it by the sound of the engine. From inside the chopper, King had also recognized the warden's voice when he'd greeted Evans a few seconds earlier.

"Come on down," Murdoch said. "I've got the Jeep. I'm surprised to see you here, but whatever you want to talk about, we might as well do it in the comfort of my office. I'll order some food from the cafeteria. They do okay with it when they know it's for me."

"I'll stay here," Evans said. "Not interested in a hostage situation."

"What are you talking about?" Murdoch said.

"Ten or 20 guards under your employ and a private game you've been playing with government assets. You've got a small army at your disposal, and I'm not interested in war. So get on the helicopter. I'm here to arrest you."

Evans motioned for King, who moved forward to the helicopter bay and stood beside Evans and looked down on Murdoch.

Murdoch flinched, but other than that, he did a good job of hiding surprise.

"King," Murdoch said. "Crazy seeing you here. I think you owe me and your dad a good explanation of why you went off the island."

"Because I had to escape last night," King said. Enjoying this. "You know. After I pepper sprayed you and hit you with an EID and duct taped around the puke on your clothes. Let me tell you, it felt good. But not as good as this."

The Jeep was 50 yards behind Murdoch. Gleaming in the sunshine.

Evans said, "Murdoch, I'm not happy. We wired the kid for sound at the hospital. Ten minutes after he calls you, he gets taken. Then there's the conversation you had with him later about the Macbook Air. I recorded that too. Nobody else but you ordered that hit. Nobody else but you had someone in place at the hospital."

"Frankly," Murdoch said. "I have no idea what you're talking about. And if I did, I doubt any of it would stand up in court."

"You won't be seeing court. You won't get a lawyer. I've got the full weight of Homeland Security behind me. We're not talking felony here. You've essentially committed domestic terrorism. That means you're going to disappear into one of our camps."

"Because of a kid with crazy stories?"

"Because of your not-so-secret-anymore bank account. Once we began looking, it didn't take long to find. You're going to have a tough time explaining the $4 million in there unless you want to get on the chopper now and get it over with."

"You want all this public? How the CIA set up games on the island?"

"You think that's going to be your protection? Think again. And listen to what I just said. Nothing's going public. We're taking you to Guantanamo. Or somewhere else. And you're going to be lost among a lot of terrorists who were caught trying to blow up the United States."

"Not going to happen," Murdoch said.

Evans snapped at Murdoch. "No games, okay? This kid here showed me some interesting video this morning. Looks like you've been sneaking trophy hunters onto the island. Now is not the time and place to argue this. I'm ordering you onto this chopper."

Murdoch backed away slightly, toward his Jeep. He unclipped a walkie-talkie from his belt. He lifted it to his mouth. "We've got a situation here. I want ten men at the helipad. And a pilot for my chopper."

"Better counter that order," Evans said.

"No," Murdoch said. "Like you made clear. No games. And you're right. I do have a private army."

"You don't have time to organize a getaway," Evans answered. "I'm sure you planned for a situation like this. You're thinking that all you need to do is get on the other chopper and make it to the mainland. But I planned for this too. You have until I get to three to counter the order you just gave."

Murdoch reached behind his back and pulled out a pistol. "Wrong."

Evans spoke calmly. Not to Murdoch, but to the pilot. "Take out the Jeep."

King hadn't given much thought to armaments. Or the capability of the Huey. Or the fact that Evans would have foreseen a situation like this and given some contingency orders ahead of time. Until that moment, King didn't know that Hueys had weapons mounted on the sides.

After a small whirring of an electric motor, there was a crack from somewhere outside the chopper. Like a crack of thunder.

Almost instantly, the Jeep disappeared in a bright flashing roar that sent shock waves toward the helicopter.

Cool, King thought.

Murdoch spun his head to the diversion.

He spun his head back to Evans, lifting the pistol to chest level. "Are you nuts?" Murdoch shouted above the sound of flames.

"Just seriously angry." Murdoch probably didn't hear Evans, but King did.

Evans ignored the pistol, raised his hand, and made a circular motion with his finger.

"I repeat," Evans said. "You have to the count of three to put down that weapon."

The commandos all stepped into sight at the bay of the helicopter. They moved forward, still standing inside, assault weapons raised and pointing down on Murdoch, forming a protective block of Kevlar vests in front of Evans and King.

"One," Evans said, calling over the shoulders of his commandos. "These guys are good. They'll hunt down every one of your men."

Murdoch hesitated.

"Two," Evans said.

Murdoch staggered and looked at his shoulder. A couple darts had appeared. King had no idea which commando had fired the darts.

Murdoch coughed once. Twice. Then fell to his knees.

"Two?" King asked.

"They always wait for the three count," Evans answered. "Get them on two, never on three. You'll note how well it works out that way."

CHAPTER 49

Three of them. Walking through the prison corridors. King. Evans. And Mack.

King had never been inside the high-security perimeters of the prison. Of course, until an hour earlier, he had never seen a rocket launcher from a Huey gunship obliterate a Jeep Wrangler—or as Samantha would have said, *ovliterate*. Hard to believe why he was walking through the prison, just as it was hard to believe that elite commandos had been sent on a search and capture mission on the same terrain they'd used on different occasions for hunting down felons in total secrecy.

A skirmish was taking place on the island as the SOGs tracked down all of Murdoch's men. But that was just a cleanup operation. The renegade guards were outnumbered, out-armed, and out-trained. It was a formality.

Inside the prison, however, it was a different matter. There were still questions that needed answering. For example, was Blake Watt still alive?

✳

The concrete floor had been painted gray and gleamed beneath florescent lights. The corridors were wide, the ceilings high. At first glance, there should have been nothing oppressive about it.

The silence, however, seemed heavy.

And with each successive security checkpoint, King felt as if they were descending into the depths of a mine. Each checkpoint consisted of thick Plexiglas and locks that opened only at the computer commands of a guard who sat behind bulletproof glass at a bank of monitors.

King thought of Mack entering this oppressive environment and enduring it for eight to ten hours every day, and once again he realized how much his perspective needed to shift. King had always viewed his dad from a selfish perspective, seeing him as a protector and provider and rule maker and judge and enforcer of rules. This was another reminder that his dad was more than "Dad," that Mack was someone like King, a person with struggles and hopes and dreams and doubts.

But thinking about that just reminded King of the secret money stashed in a bank account that he'd accessed on Mack's computer. And the knot in King's stomach seemed to grow like a malignant tumor.

None of them talked. It wasn't the place for chitchat, and Mack was leading them with the certainty of an experienced guide. The only sounds were their footsteps on the painted concrete.

They reached one more checkpoint. King glanced at yet another pane of bulletproof glass but saw no guard. Just the regular bank of monitors.

Mack stopped and pointed at a door, talking to Evans. "You're the only one authorized at this point."

Evans nodded and held a card in front of a magnetic sensor, and the door slid open from left to right. It was at least six inches thick and moved slowly until it disappeared completely.

Like the other checkpoints, this guardroom was hardly larger than a walk-in closet. Unlike the other checkpoints, this one had no guard.

"Ten cells in this final corridor," Mack said. "In theory, none are occupied. None of our shifts are assigned to this area."

Inside the small guardroom, the monitors were dull black. Mack hit a few buttons, and one by one, the monitors appeared to wake.

The first two monitors showed an empty corridor from different perspectives, just like the one King had seen in the video on the Macbook Air. And the tumor in his stomach swelled to another level of pain. What was his dad's secret? How had he been involved? King had no intention of betraying his father to Evans, but how could King ever trust his dad again?

The third monitor showed the interior of a cell. Steel bed with thin mattress along one wall. Steel sink on opposite wall. Steel toilet in a corner. An area smaller than a bedroom. No windows. No prisoner.

The fourth monitor was identical. As were the fifth and sixth and the remaining four after that. All the cells were empty.

Mack took a deep breath. "Rumors were wrong. We'd heard there was an off-limits prisoner back here."

"Or," Evans said, "Murdoch got a sense that something was going wrong and moved the kid before we landed with the Huey."

Which would mean, King thought, either that Blake Watt had been dead all along or that he had been moved and was now dead.

"My vote?" Mack said. "We go back through the prison cell by cell and check each one until we know for sure."

King asked a question. "How easy would it be to set up fake video feeds to one of these monitors? I mean, you could have one camera in cell five, for example, feeding two monitors at the same time. Because if I was Murdoch and I didn't want anyone to see someone in this wing, that's the first thing I'd do."

"Smart," Evans said. "Maybe someday you want to work for me?"

CHAPTER 50

King, Mack, and Evans moved into the final corridor of the prison and stopped at the first cell.

The door had a horizontal slot chest high. Like a place to drop mail. Not even big enough to slide a hand through the opening. It was shielded with clear plastic. Nothing could get through anyway.

Below it was another slot, this one wide enough to slide a tray.

"Normal procedure?" Evans asked. Holding up his EID.

King didn't understand the question, but Mack obviously did.

"First we check the video to learn the prisoner's location in the cell."

A small monitor mounted near the ceiling showed what they had seen on the monitors at the checkpoint—an empty cell.

"Let's assume it's not empty," Evans said. "If Murdoch was hiding a kid down here, maybe he had others as well. Convicts. Special punishment."

"Anywhere else in the prison, we always give them 30 seconds to take the position on the far wall where we can see them. Facing the wall. On their knees. Hands locked behind their heads. Then we enter."

Mack pressed a small button on the outside of the wall. A clear beeping sound reached them. Mack peered through the slot. "Nobody in position."

"Could someone be hiding up against the wall on this side?" Evans asked.

"When it happens," Mack said, "we see them on the video. That's when we go for our gas masks and lob a canister of tear gas into the cell. Prisoners only try that once."

"Except here, if the video is doctored and someone is inside." Evans held up his EID pistol. "I spent ten years in SOG. You learned to assume the worst and protect against it. Or you didn't survive."

"Then we slide the door open, and go in one at a time," Mack said, holding up his own EID pistol. "I'll go in first. Keep some distance. Anything happens, make sure you don't hit the wrong target."

"If you're trying to insult me, congratulations," Evans said. "It's not my first rodeo."

"And that's why you know you talk things out as a team before you make a move. Even if it means stating the obvious."

"Fair enough," Evans said. "Apologies. I'm ready."

Seeing his dad in a new perspective wasn't getting old for King. He was proud of his dad's coolness and strength. Fully an equal to some guy from SOG with killer eyes.

Mack lifted his plastic card to the magnetic sensor, and the door slid open in the same way as the one at the checkpoint.

King was holding his breath, half expecting a prisoner to leap out in a surprise attack.

Nothing.

King drew air into his lungs.

They repeated this five more times, and each time, King felt his stress level build and then drop as each cell proved to be empty. And again, he realized he was getting a taste of what his dad had faced each day working at the prison.

At the seventh cell, after Mack pressed the buzzer and looked inside, he spoke with a flatness that King knew was just about Mack's only outward betrayal of fury.

"He's there," Mack said. He backed away from the observation slot.

"The kid?" Evans asked.

Mack nodded. "Taking the position. Murdoch had him here the entire time. Taught him to behave like a con. And the kid is cuffed. Any idea how terrified this kid must be? And what it did to his parents, believing he'd drowned?"

"It's over now," Evans said. "At least we have that."

"Not quite," King said. "Mr. Evans, you're going to remember your promise, right? Door closed and complete privacy. I get five minutes alone with Blake."

CHAPTER 51

Blake maintained his position as the door slid open. He was wearing a con's uniform, far too large for him. He was on his knees, his face inches away from the wall. His hands were locked behind his neck. Handcuffed. And his ankles were hobbled too.

King had expected Blake to turn when the door opened but then realized that this must have been how Murdoch trained Blake. Food once a day? Occasional visits from Murdoch? In the brief time it took for King to wait for the door to slide back shut again, he imagined how horrible it would have been for Blake. He was just a kid. Locked away from the world. Solitude. Depending on the man who had captured him for something as simple as food or conversation.

"Blake," King said. "It's over. We're taking you out. Back to your parents."

Blake remained rigid against the wall. "Murdoch with you? Is this a trick?"

"Look for yourself," King said. "It's me."

"I heard the door slide shut behind you," Blake said, still facing the wall. "That doesn't sound like freedom to me. I'm sorry if what I did got you here. Murdoch, let him go. If you do, I'll tell you the rest of what you need. If you don't, you can burn me a hundred times and I won't give you anything else about the computer."

"Was it that bad? That you're scared to turn around?"

"Any idea how much a cigarette burn can hurt? But I'm not scared. I'm mad. And if this is a trick and Murdoch is with you, he's going to light a cigarette for you as punishment if I make a wrong move."

King felt like a collapsing balloon, he was so sad for Blake. King moved forward and put a gentle hand on Blake's shoulder.

"The door is closed because I wanted time alone with you. That was the bargain I made with the CIA."

"Truth? I won't turn around and see Murdoch standing behind you with an EID in one hand and an unlit cigarette in the other? You have no idea how much I hate the smell of cigarette smoke."

"Truth," King said. "It worked—the dead man's switch."

Slowly, without turning away from the wall, Blake lifted his hand-cuffed wrists back over his head and dropped them in front of him, below his waist. He still didn't turn. Instead, he sagged into the wall until his forehead touched. His shoulders began to shake.

King knew that Blake was sobbing soundlessly.

King sat on the edge of the bed on the wall that was at a right angle to Blake. He waited for Blake to compose himself.

It took a few minutes. King was okay with that. Evans had promised he wasn't going to open the door until King knocked.

Blake finally lifted his head and made eye contact with King. His face was pale, and he looked shrunken. His eyes were red. Tears streamed down along his nose and joined long strings of mucus.

"Dude, I was so worried for you," Blake said. "Murdoch told me if I didn't get him the computer passwords, he'd take you and MJ down."

"That's a lot of snot," King said. "Sink and faucet in here work, right?"

Blake laughed.

King took that as a good sign.

King waited while Blake washed his face. Blake looked marginally better as the water dried.

"You ready for a question?" King asked. "Before the door opens for us?"

"Just one?"

"A guy named Evans is outside. He's CIA. He'll have plenty of questions for you. But I only need to know one thing. And I want the truth. You owe it to me."

"King, I didn't know who else to send those emails to. I mean, you're the only one I figured who had the brains and guts to do what it took."

"One question," King said. To King, it was the only question that mattered. "Did you put the money in my dad's bank account?"

CHAPTER 52

"It's the money that did this," Blake said. He wiped at his nose with the sleeve of his con uniform. "First, it's how I began to track things. It was such an easy hack, getting into the prison servers. I used the iPhone to access my own PayPal account and pay a no-contract carrier for the cell phone data. Then I ordered myself a computer. Once I had the computer, I used the iPhone to get Internet access. When I started hacking around, I found that Murdoch had millions in offshore accounts."

"I know all of that," King said. "I want to know why my dad has a quarter million in his savings account."

"I found the money first," Blake said. "Murdoch's money. I began to wonder how he got it, and that led to everything else. I was safe until I moved some of the money to different accounts. I just wanted to mess with him. That's how he caught me. When he noticed the money missing, he hired a hacker to trace me. I had covered nearly all my tracks but not enough. I was only worried about government computer geeks. They're idiots. I didn't expect Murdoch to go on the forums and find the best of the best."

Blake trembled, something that shook his entire body. "He promised he was going to let me go as soon as I returned the money. I didn't believe him. Here's the funny thing. I set up the dead man's switch to use as a safeguard, but at first, I didn't even have to use that on Murdoch to stay alive. Instead, I found out he couldn't kill me until he got his money back."

Blake lifted his sleeve, and King saw small circular blisters on Blake's arm.

"I held out as long as I could," Blake said. "And finally, when he said he was going to hurt my parents and then my friends, I told him about the money. As soon as he recovered it, he began to tie me up to take me outside. He told me that was all he needed before leaving the island, that he'd been getting ready to live a new life somewhere in South America. To stay alive longer, I told him about the dead man's switch. I told him if he didn't keep me alive, a two-week switch would be triggered. I didn't tell him it had already been triggered."

"When did you tell him about the dead man's switch?" King asked.

"A couple nights ago. I think. It's hard to keep track of time in here."

That made sense to King. After that, Murdoch had begun watching King and MJ more closely. They were Blake's friends, the ones Blake would probably use for help. And when King entered the abandoned prison at night, it was confirmed for Murdoch. King shuddered at the memory of sitting in the back of the Jeep with Mack up front. Mack knew something bad would happen if he allowed Murdoch to take King. And King had nearly chosen Murdoch over his own father.

"All I want to know about is the money in my dad's account," King said.

"I had to lie to you," Blake said. "I knew that all along as I was setting up the dead man's switch. That if I didn't lie to you and give you a good enough reason to keep looking for answers, I wouldn't have a chance. And I knew you and your dad were tight. I knew that about the only way I could motivate you was by threatening your dad. Dude, to me it was a game. Until it became real. If I had known that someday I'd actually need the dead man's switch, I wouldn't have involved you."

"I understand," King said. "Really."

King had lied to MJ to get him to help. It was no different from what Blake had done. And King wasn't sure he would have endured cigarette burns as long as Blake had endured them, keeping King's involvement secret as long as possible.

Blake's face didn't show belief that King was cool with it.

"Blake," King said, "you have blister circles up and down your arms because you were trying to protect me and MJ and your family. I don't know if I would have had that courage."

Blake gave a small smile.

"What I really care about," King said, "is the money in my dad's bank account. Was it you?"

"I faked the surveillance footage. Made your dad look guilty."

King took a deep, satisfied breath. It felt like the first time, really, he'd been able to breathe since the night in the old prison, seeing that surveillance footage. And the bank account.

"The money."

"You know the answer," Blake said. "I just put it there so you'd think you had to protect your dad by searching for me until you got here."

CHAPTER 53

Ella's iPhone buzzed in King's pocket.

He was in the hospital room with Mack, waiting for a report from Ella's physician. King glanced at the screen and saw that it was a Face-Time request from Johnson.

"Be right back," King said to Mack.

Mack nodded. He was at the bed, holding Ella's hand.

King connected the call and stepped into the hallway.

"Kinger," MJ said, his grin filling the screen.

"MJ. You okay?"

"Let me think. CIA lets us do a three-way split on the funds Watt had moved from Murdoch into your dad's account as long as we promise to use the money for university. Hmmm. Yeah, I'm okay."

Since busting Blake from the cell, Evans had arranged for a military jet to bring Blake's parents back to Joint Base Lewis-McChord. Joyful reunion was an understatement.

The base was also where Evans had taken King, Mack, MJ, and MJ's parents for an intense debriefing that had lasted long into the evening. Evans had done the carrot and stick routine. He'd outlined the dangers of going public about the CIA military exercises on the island, and he made the deal about the funds that Mack had no idea were in the bank account hidden in his Vacations folders in his emails.

"How about you?" MJ asked. "Your mom. Any news?"

"Waiting right now," King said.

The background of the FaceTime call showed that MJ was likely in one of the drab rooms where enlisted men bunked.

"So why'd you text me to call?" MJ asked. "I thought this chat would be about your mom."

Confession time.

"Last night," King said, "Evans was so intense, I never found the time to tell you something I needed to tell you."

MJ grinned. "Like you lied to me about how if I didn't help you, my dad would be exposed for some horrible crime? Come on, think I couldn't figure that out last night as we put the pieces together for Evans?"

"You don't look mad," King said. "I feel horrible about this. We're best friends. I lied to you."

"We're cool," MJ said. He did stop smiling though. "I mean, to protect my dad, I would have done the same if I were you. And if you want the truth, I was kind of hoping I'd be able to prove my dad was doing something wrong, and I feel guilty about it."

King's turn. "Huh?"

"We've been fighting like crazy. He's always yelling at me, trying to tell me what to do. Everything. Manners at the dinner table. When to do my homework. How to do my homework. Then a few minutes ago, I realized something about him that made me feel worse than you might feel for lying to me."

"Yeah?"

"Dad really majors in the minors," MJ said. "Nitpicks all the time. But I didn't realize that when it came to something big, he minors in the majors."

MJ grinned again. "When the CIA showed up and started to explain that somehow I was involved in this, I thought my dad would go crazy on me. I mean, if chewing with your mouth open at the table gets criticism, how about doing something that brings in the CIA?"

MJ's grin widened. "Just the opposite. Dad put his arm around my shoulder and said that no matter what, he had my back. That the CIA was going to get some serious hurt if they tried messing with me. Cool, huh? I love that guy."

"I know the feeling," King said.

MJ pulled the phone farther back so that King could see that MJ was holding out his knuckle again for a fist bump.

"Air bump, dude," MJ said.

"MJ, no. That's so grade school." MJ loved to bump knuckles, complete with the starburst.

"Kinger, last one, I promise."

MJ always said that.

King pushed the iPhone away so that he and MJ could bump knuckles by video, and sure enough, out came the wriggly finger star dust as MJ pulled his hand away after contact.

So the two of them were good, and King had his confession out of the way.

All that remained now was figuring out if Ella would ever come out of the coma.

*

Mack and King stood when Dr. Jennifer Brennan entered the room. She was frowning. King didn't like that.

Dr. Brennan had short hair, brown with frosted blonde streaks. She wore the hospital standards and had a stethoscope hanging around her neck. She had a clipboard and frowned again as she looked at it and then looked up at Mack and King.

She didn't waste time on any pleasantries.

"What we've found," she said, "is that yes, there are traces of illegal pharmaceuticals in your mother's blood, matching the traces found in the IV bag."

She glanced up from the clipboard. "I promise you we will investigate this thoroughly, and I suspect that means the end of the career of one of my colleagues. I've been instructed to inform you that the hospital had nothing to do with this, and any legal action should be directed against your mother's attending physician."

King felt his heart bump. In a good way. Brennan's frown was a selfish frown. Brennan's first concern had been politics. Could it be that King's guess about Jerome had been correct?

"Look," Mack said. "Right now would be a good time for you to talk to us about Ella, not about whatever you're trying to do to cover your collective hind ends."

That got through.

Brennan looked directly at Mack, bowed her head, and then lifted it again.

She shook her head and gave them a wry grin, and then she blew out a breath. "You know, sometimes I need a sharp reminder like that. I apologize. And I have good news."

King felt his heart bump again. If Jerome had been working for Murdoch, and if Murdoch had been using Ella's coma as leverage against Mack until Murdoch could make an escape to South America...

"Mr. King," Brennan said. "The blood tests show that yes, your wife has been artificially maintained in a coma. What I'd like to know is how you came to this conclusion."

No way were Mack and King permitted to divulge this. Not by the confidentiality agreement signed for the CIA.

"Desperation," Mack said. "How long?"

"Till the drugs in her system wear off?" Brennan said. She smiled again, and it took years off her face. "I'd suggest both of you sit by the bed and wait. It could be any minute now. Do me a favor and send a nurse for me when it happens. We'll need to run some tests, but once she wakes up, your wife can be released from the hospital."

That's when King heard two words that brought tears to his eyes.

"Mack?" Ella said. "King?"

They were family again.

END NOTES

Yes. There is a game called Dead Man's Switch. Yes, it does involve prisoners hunting government operatives as a real-life training exercise. Go to www.deadmans-switch.com to learn more.

*

Yes. McNeil Island is real. So is the location, in Puget Sound, just west of Seattle-Tacoma. So is the prison on the island. The original prison was opened in 1875 and closed in 2011, and the abandoned prison remains. The houses on the island exist as described. As does the reservoir in the center of the island.

The only families there are families of prison employees. The island has no ferry service, no police force, no stores. Three-quarters of the island is wildlife refuge. It is the only prison island still in existence in the United States.

Although some fictional changes have been made in this novel, as of the writing of *Dead Man's Switch*, some prisoners deemed unfit to be returned to society are still living on the island.

*

Yes. Joint Base Lewis-McChord sits just south of Tacoma, a location that gives it easy access to deep water ports, and it has its own airfield. JBLM is also the location for the 201st Battlefield Surveillance Brigade. According to Wikipedia, this BfSB…

rapidly provides deployable all-source predictive intelligence, electronic warfare intelligence, reconnaissance and surveillance, target acquisition, battle damage assessment, command and control warfare, and broad bandwidth communications support to I Corps. It trains for and prepares to operate in both Joint and Combined environments in support of worldwide contingencies. The brigade concentrates on providing a shared battlefield situational awareness, and ensures the direct downlink of national and theater level intelligence through full spectrum operations assets as part of a multi-disciplined intelligence collection, surveillance and reconnaissance unit to an Army Corps or a designated Joint Task Force.[1]

＊

Yes. The drug metyrapone exists. It does function to erase short-term traumatic memories. It is still in the experimental stage.

＊

Yes. There are many websites devoted to the dead man's switch concept, including www.deadmansswitch.net.

＊

And yes, of course, the Central Intelligence Agency exists. As does the Special Operations Group.

The CIA is openly acknowledged as one of the United States' intelligence-gathering organizations.

Within the CIA exists the National Clandestine Service (NCS), which is one of the four main components of the CIA and "serves as

---

1 http://en.wikipedia.org/wiki/201st_Battlefield_Surveillance_Brigade

the clandestine arm of the Central Intelligence Agency (CIA) and the national authority for the coordination, de-confliction, and evaluation of clandestine operations across the Intelligence Community of the United States."[2]

NCS is responsible for the Special Activities Division (SAD), which is responsible for covert operations, and within SAD is the more secretive special operations force of the United States, the Special Operations Group.

The SOG selects operatives from the elite of the elite—from Delta Force, DEVGRU (SEAL Team Six), the 24th Special Tactics Squadron, and other special operations forces from within the US military.

> SOG Paramilitary Operations Officers account for a healthy majority of Distinguished Intelligence Cross and Intelligence Star recipients during any given conflict or incident which elicits CIA involvement…SAD/SOG operatives also account for the majority of the names displayed on the Memorial Wall at CIA headquarters indicating that the agent died while on active duty, most likely during the execution of a covert operation or other high-risk assignment in accordance with the founding principles of Special Activities Division.[3]

A 1976 presidential edict makes it illegal for the CIA to engage in political assassinations, but following the directives after 9/11, there is debate on the legality of using special forces to hunt terrorists.

✳

As for the reality of a base where SOG operatives' skills are honed for real-world operations by the exercise of hunting and being hunted by dangerous humans, some would declare this to be nothing but speculative fiction.

---

2 https://www.cia.gov/offices-of-cia/clandestine-service/

3 http://en.wikipedia.org/wiki/Special_Activities_Division

To learn more about Harvest House books and
to read sample chapters, visit our website:

www.harvesthousepublishers.com

HARVEST HOUSE PUBLISHERS
EUGENE, OREGON